YANKEE SPY

A Union Girl in Richmond during the Peninsular Campaign

Young Americans Series #3

By

Maureen Stack Sappéy

WHITE MANE KIDS

This White Mane Books publication
was printed by
Beidel Printing House, Inc.
63 West Burd Street
Shippensburg, PA 17257-0152 USA

In respect for the scholarship contained herein, the acid-free paper used in this book meets the guidelines for permanence and durability of the Committee on Production Guidelines for Book Longevity of the Council on Library Resources.

For a complete list of available publications
please write
White Mane Books
Division of White Mane Publishing Company, Inc.
P.O. Box 152
Shippensburg, PA 17257-0152 USA

Library of Congress Cataloging-in-Publication Data
Sappey, Maureen Stack, 1952-
    Yankee spy : a Union girl in Richmond during the Peninsular Campaign / by Maureen Stack Sappey.
        p.   cm. -- (Young American series : #3)
    Summary: Louisa, a Union patriot, finds a way to help the Army of the Potomac as it fights its way toward the Confederate capital in the Peninsular Campaign of 1862.
    ISBN 1-57249-135-3 (alk. paper)
    1. Peninsular Campaign, 1862--Juvenile fiction. 2. Richmond (Va.)--History--Civil War, 1861-1865--Juvenile fiction.
    [1. Peninsular Campaign, 1862--Fiction. 2. Richmond (Va.)--History--Civil War, 1861-1865--Fiction. 3. United States--History--Civil War, 1861-1865--Fiction. 4. Spies--Fiction.] I. Title.
    II. Series.
PZ7.S2388Yan   1998
[Fic]--dc21   98-24051
                                                                        CIP
                                                                        AC

PRINTED IN THE UNITED STATES OF AMERICA

DEDICATION

With great love, I dedicate this book to
my twin daughters, Bridget and Kathleen,
whose faces reveal the beauty of their hearts.

CONTENTS

ACKNOWLEDGMENTS

Writers of history are merely interpreters of historical facts. Those facts are gathered by historians who disagree about their findings as often as they agree. This story, which is based on my own interpretation of historical facts, was drawn from periodicals, maps, books and personal interviews. I took great care to present, as truthfully as possible, the facts concerning Generals Robert E. Lee, Joseph E. Johnston, and George B. McClellan, President Jefferson Davis and his wife Varina, the spies Timothy Webster and his associate, Mrs. Hattie Lawton, the city and citizens of Richmond, and the soldiers of the North and South. Julia and Louisa Holmes, James Hamilton, Dr. Hugh Ryle, his sister Charleen and her daughter, Ashley, are fictitious characters.

In particular, seven books proved invaluable as research tools. Earnest B. Furgurson's masterful book, *Ashes of Glory: Richmond at War* should be read by anyone who wishes to better understand the horrible consequences for a city shadowed by war. Three books about Civil War spies offered me keen insight into the world of espionage: *Spies, Scouts and Raiders: Irregular Operations* edited by Henry Anatole Grumwald, *Secret Missions of the Civil War* by Philip Van Doren Stern, and *Spies of the Confederacy* by John Bakeless. In addition, three other books detailed General George B. McClellan's failed campaign up the Peninsula of Virginia: *Battle Chronicles of the Civil War* by James M. McPherson, *Voices of the Civil War* by Richard Wheeler, and *The Civil War: Forward to Richmond, McClellan's Peninsular Campaign*, edited by Thomas H. Flaherty.

As always, I leaned heavily on experts in the related fields of American history, medicine, war science, psychology, and professional writing. Those experts must be noted and thanked.

Mrs. Joy Maine and Mr. Michael Edman, the illustrators of this book, for creating beautiful interpretations of my words.

Mr. David Madden, the director of The United States Civil War Center, Louisiana State University, Baton Rouge, Louisiana, and his assistant, Ms. Leah Wood, for their suggestions and enthusiasm about my writings about the Civil War.

Dr. Patrick J. Shanahan, a physician and writer, for his expert advice about the lifestyles and medical practices of the Civil War surgeon, and for his insight about the form of insanity suffered by the character, Charleen Beecham.

Mr. Bill Blake, a true gentleman renown as a living history re-enactor with the Second Maryland Infantry, Company G, CSA, and as a Civil War lecturer, screen writer, and film actor, for his careful consideration of both the factual and fictional accounts in this book.

Mrs. Jean Rheingrover, the professional children's writer, for her astute comments about the techniques of writing employed in this text.

Ms. Beverly Kuhn, of Beidel Printing House, and Mr. Harold Collier of White Mane Books, for their collaboration and professionalism in the production of this book and the other books in my series.

And as always, my supreme gratitude to my husband Steve, our children John, Brian, Bridget and Kathleen, and my dad and stepmother, John and Barbara Stack, for their kind interest in my writing.

CHAPTER ONE

Julia wept softly as our carriage moved out into the street. Nothing else could be said to comfort her though, for my words had failed to console her. Instead, I cradled her hand in mine as we looked out at the sleeping city.

Our carriage passed darkened windows and closed doors; here and there a policeman walked his rounds, but otherwise the streets of Washington were empty. Such emptiness seemed unfamiliar and strange to us, for we had grown accustomed to streets crowded with thousands of soldiers and horses and army wagons. That morning the streets seemed almost barren, for on the previous day, the twenty-seventh of March 1862, General George McClellan marched his army out of the city towards Alexandria, Virginia. Why he did so, no one knew—for once the general's plans remained secretive. Washington's newspapers could only speculate about the final destination of our army.

The train station was deserted too; in the silence we heard the echo of our heels as we hurried across the platform floor. Julia bought a ticket for New York City and after tucking it inside her glove, she slipped her arm through mine and we walked slowly towards the train. All at once, my sister paused and smiling sadly she said, "Dearest Louisa, this is the very spot where James kissed me. His kiss captured my heart . . . my heart still belo—"

The blast of the train's whistle drowned out Julia's last words, but I understood what she would have said—that her heart still belonged to James.

For the past several weeks my sister had haunted our letter box, wondering why James' daily letters had ceased, when she received a long letter from his mother. Mrs. Hamilton wrote that on March 9 her son had been aboard the Union's ironclad ship, *Monitor*, when it had battled the Confederacy's ironclad, *Virginia*—the ship our Union knew as the *Merrimack*. At battle's end an exploding shell blinded James and he was moved to his family's home in New York City for treatment. Mrs. Hamilton wrote that the doctors couldn't explain James' blindness, for his eyes appeared undamaged. And she wrote that he had withdrawn into a world of self-pity, and that he spent his days sitting in a darkened room. Knowing of James' affection for my sister, Mrs. Hamilton implored Julia to visit in the hope her presence might dispel the gloom that had settled around her son's heart. Julia packed at once.

A porter helped Julia carry her luggage onto the train, and moments later I saw her lovely face through the window of a car; although she waved cheerfully, her smile revealed the sorrow that shadowed her heart. For a brief moment Julia looked younger than her age of sixteen years and in that same moment I felt aged, years older than my own seventeen years. Often, since our parents' death, I felt such moments in which I thought of myself as my sister's elder, as her guide and protector. And yet, I knew I was powerless to shield her heart from life's sorrows. I returned Julia's smile and after her train disappeared I crossed the platform towards Joseph who had turned the horses around.

The streets were no longer deserted; the first light of day revealed merchants sweeping their store fronts and women carrying baskets on their arms and boys tossing newspapers at doorsteps. Not a soldier was to be seen, although it was said that part of the Federal army had remained behind to protect our city from Confederate invasion.

In the silence of that early morning I thought of Adam. Often, in unguarded moments, I remembered the emerald-green of his eyes or the sound of his voice, but I no longer wept when those memories came over me. Don't judge me as coldhearted; instead, know me as someone whose heart had been numbed by the War.

And yet, though my heart felt numb, I thought of Adam and all at once I had to know General McClellan's reason for marching his vast army to Alexandria. I had to know if he had finally found the courage to lead our army into battle—I had to know if my beloved Adam had not died in vain.

I bid Joseph to drive me at once to the port city of Alexandria on the Virginian side of the Potomac River, and he snapped his whip and quickened the horses' step over the cobbled streets.

After some time Joseph slowed the horses to a walk, for we had entered the muddy road that led to the wooden bridge known as Chain Bridge. As we drew closer I noticed that Union soldiers patrolled both sides of the bridge, and I wondered about that as two soldiers ran towards my carriage.

One of the soldiers, a brutish-looking man with a grizzly beard, pointed his weapon at Joseph and shouted at him to pull over. Puzzled, I leaned forward and asked the soldier his purpose in delaying my carriage, but he gave no answer. Instead, he turned his musket towards my face and ordered me out of my carriage.

CHAPTER TWO

The soldier nodded towards a tent pitched at the far corner of the bridge and though he said nothing, I understood to follow him. Inside the tent the light was dim and the air smelled like wet dog hair. A sergeant and a colonel stood behind a rickety table; both men wore grim expressions as though they had drunk sour milk. Behind them, on a low stool, sat a plain-looking woman with such a sharp nose and pointed chin that she resembled a witch in a child's fairy tale.

The officers sat down without offering me a seat and I knew then that I was not in the company of gentlemen. I said, "I wish to leave now."

"You can leave when we are through questioning you," the colonel replied.

A fury swept over me and I demanded to know what crime I had committed to have been ordered so rudely from my carriage. However, instead of answering my question, the colonel asked my purpose in crossing Chain Bridge at such an early hour.

Startled by the colonel's question, I hesitated and my hesitation caused him to narrow his eyes at me as though I were a criminal. He said, "I am asking you for the final time, miss . . . what is your purpose in driving to Virginia?"

I replied, "My purpose, sir, is none of your business, but if you must know . . . I wish to learn the reason General McClellan has marched his army to Alexandria."

"Why?" the colonel asked in the dullest, flattest voice I have ever heard.

I thought again of my beloved Adam, but as I looked into the colonel's bloodshot eyes I knew he would never understand my reasons for driving to Alexandria. A man as vulgar as he wouldn't understand my need to know if Adam's death had had purpose and meaning. So I merely said, "My reasons are private, sir."

The colonel's expression hardened and he pushed a paper and pen across the table and ordered me to add my name and address to a long list of other names and addresses. He pulled the paper back and reading my name he said, "Miss Louisa Holmes, since you refuse to answer my questions I must assume that you are guilty of espionage for the Confederacy."

I felt the blood rushing into my face and with great effort I steadied the anger in my voice before saying, "How dare you accuse me of being a spy. Last summer, my betrothed, Major Adam Sorenson, fought in the Battle of Bull Run. His wounds proved mortal . . . I would never betray the very nation he died for."

The colonel was unimpressed by my admission. In his flat voice he said, "In recent weeks traitors have attempted to cross this bridge . . . female traitors who thought their curls and fine gowns would allow them to pass without suspicion. They thought wrong. I suspect everyone. Yesterday a lady, not unlike yourself, wanted to cross Chain Bridge, but she, too, refused to answer my questions. She was searched and we found military secrets hidden in a hollow ring that she claimed was her wedding band. Her intention was to hand the information over to Jeff Davis, but she has been imprisoned.

"Miss Holmes, since you, too, refuse to answer my questions, I must search you."

I felt myself go white with sudden fear of his disgusting hands on my person, but he and the sergeant suddenly stood and passed through the door; they lowered the flap behind them which darkened the tent even more. I stiffened, too frightened to move, as the witchy woman came towards me.

She ordered me out of my dress and then my hoops and I watched in humiliation as she patted the hem of my gown and examined the heels of my shoes. After I had dressed again, she ordered me to remove my net, so as to explore my hair with her bony fingers. She then examined my rings and bracelet and finally satisfied that I was not a treasonous spy, she gestured towards the flap of the tent and I rushed outside.

Poor Joseph had suffered his search in public. When I came upon him he was sitting on the ground pulling on his socks and boots. Behind him, a soldier was examining the cushions and lamps of my carriage while another tapped on the wheels. Of course their search uncovered nothing villainous—all they found was one of Julia's hat pins. After some time a provost guard scribbled out a bridge pass; Joseph tucked the pass into the brim of his hat, helped me into the carriage and with an angry snap of his reins he drove us over Chain Bridge before turning south towards Virginia.

CHAPTER THREE

Joseph parked the carriage under the branches of a leafless oak. Before me stretched the docks of Alexandria where thousands of soldiers were lined up along the murky waters of the Potomac. The river was dotted with ships and boats; hundreds of vessels with white sails or paddle-wheels or chimneys belching black smoke.

I sat in my carriage and listened to the noises of departure: of officers barking orders; of thousands of shoes as soldiers shuffled slowly along the pier; of neighing horses; and of creaking limbers as massive cannons inched over wide gangplanks into the waiting ships. Above those noises rose the tinny music of parade bands and the cheers and shouts of hundreds of civilians who shared my curiosity.

I suppose General McClellan should be given credit for the orderliness of his army's departure, but I disliked him with a passion because I mistrusted him. When he first appeared in Washington I was amused by his reputation as the Young Napoleon, but after

observing him at receptions and during those count-
less parades he preferred instead of battles I came to
one conclusion—that General McClellan was a vain,
egotistical man. Indeed I had heard disturbing rumors
that he considered President Lincoln a fool and
dreamed of becoming Dictator of America. So, although I applauded General McClellan's flawless departure of his giant army, I still mistrusted him.

As I watched the spectacle before me I didn't
notice that a gentleman had approached my carriage;
his voice startled me.

"Good morning," he repeated and I murmured a
greeting.

He was a tall gentleman of perhaps thirty years
and quite handsome. In fact, he bore a remarkable
resemblance to General McClellan; both had thick black
hair and curling mustaches and both had wide eyes
and generous mouths, but whereas General McClellan
was my height, this other gentleman was well over
six feet. He smiled at me, a rather sophisticated smile,
and tipping his hat he said, "Miss Holmes, I believe."

I tried to remember if we had previously met, but
apparently not for he said, "Allow me to introduce
myself. I am Dr. Andrew Gleason, physician to your
neighbors, the Murdocks. On a recent call there I noticed you sitting on your porch . . . Mrs. Murdock told
me your name."

I must admit that I took an instant dislike to Dr.
Gleason. Perhaps because of his striking resemblance
to General McClellan or perhaps because there was
something in Dr. Gleason's eyes that made me mis-
trust him, too.

To change the subject to a less personal tone, I
asked Dr. Gleason if he thought the army's departure
would be completed by noon.

He smiled at me as though I were thick-witted
and said, "Miss Holmes, it will take nearly three weeks

for McClellan's army to depart Alexandria. There are, after all, over 100,000 troops."

"Three weeks," I repeated in disbelief, and then, because he stared at me so boldly, my cheeks burned with embarrassment. His impertinent stare intensified my dislike for him, for I had the oddest notion about him. Oh, I have admitted that his face was remarkably handsome, but cruelty marked his eyes and mouth as though his comely face was a mask that concealed a sinister heart. Strange that I should think of a physician as sinister.

I looked back at the docks and wondered out loud, "Where on earth is General McClellan moving our army?"

"To Fort Monroe on the Peninsula of Virginia," Dr. Gleason answered without hesitation.

His words surprised me and turning towards him I said, "For the first time since General McClellan took command of our nation's armies, our newspapers were unable to report his plans. Supposedly, some of the general's own officers are unaware of the army's destination. May I ask how a civilian such as yourself, Dr. Gleason, could have learned the secret plans of General McClellan?"

His lips seemed to curl up when he smiled and his answer was vague: "A physician is privy to private conversations." And then he completely changed the subject by adding, "Mrs. Murdock mentioned that you own a house in Richmond. Do you know that city well?"

"Very well. Richmond was my mother's home," I replied in some confusion as to why he wanted to know.

He looked at me as though he studied me before saying, "Mrs. Murdock also mentioned that you have spoken of your desire to help end this War. Is that the truth, or the fanciful words of a beautiful lady?"

I ignored his compliment and said, "I rarely speak in jest, Dr. Gleason."

His smile deepened. "There is a way you can help end this War, Miss Holmes. May I call on you tonight to explain?"

I had no desire to see him again, but if there was some way in which I could help my nation, I would listen to anyone. I agreed to receive him at eight that evening before bidding Joseph to drive me home.

CHAPTER FOUR

The clock chimed the hour of eight when I heard loud knocking at my front door. A moment later Bessie ushered Dr. Gleason into the parlor and he took my hand and bowed his head. I indicated the chair across from mine and asked Bessie to bring the tea tray.

Bessie placed the tray before me and after she closed the door Dr. Gleason said, "I must confess I have been watching you for several months, Miss Holmes. Your reputation for loyalty to the Union is well known. What I will propose demands great loyalty, because there is danger involved."

His words startled me, but pouring out the tea I asked, "Cream?"

Dr. Gleason laughed (a rather unpleasant sound). "You surprise me, Miss Holmes, he said. "I mention danger and you mention cream. Could a lady as beautiful as you have no fear?"

Because I disliked him his compliment irritated me. Disguising the impatience in my voice I asked, "How can I be of service to our nation?"

The laughter died in his eyes as he asked, "Are you aware that the Confederacy has employed ladies from Washington to deliver military secrets to Jefferson Davis and his generals?"

Nodding, I told him of my delay that morning at Chain Bridge, and he shrugged as though my story was old news to him before asking, "Are you acquainted with Mrs. Rose Greenhow?"

I hesitated before answering: "Unfortunately, I am—you cannot imagine my shock to learn that a lady of Washington society would spy for the Confederacy. I applauded her arrest—"

"She may be executed," Dr. Gleason interrupted. "It has been learned that her spy work caused the Union's defeat at the Battle of Bull Run. Supposedly Mrs. Greenhow sent information about the movement of the Union's army to the Confederates which allowed them ample time to position their army and call in reinforcements. One could argue that Mrs. Greenhow is partly responsible for the death of every Federal at Bull Run."

My heart pounded and my hand shook so much that my cup rattled on its saucer. Could it be possible that Mrs. Greenhow—that vile traitor—was somehow responsible for Adam's death? Lifting my chin I asked, "Tell me what you wish me to do."

A smile grazed his mouth when he answered, "You can spy for our Union."

My heart pounded even louder as he continued, "If you agree, you must leave for Virginia tonight. Remain at your home in Richmond until a major in the Confederate army calls on you. His name is Major Robert Petrie—he is, in fact, a Unionist posing as a Confederate officer."

Dr. Gleason took a small box from his coat pocket. "Miss Holmes, while you're in Richmond you, too, must pose as a Confederate." He opened the box and removed a circular brooch of flattened silver decorated with a large letter, C. "The C stands for the Confederacy," he explained. "You must wear this brooch while you're in Richmond as a sign of your loyalty to the Confederate States of America. Show the brooch to Major Petrie the moment you first meet and he will recognize you as my courier."

From the same box Dr. Gleason drew out a pocket watch; it was a handsome timepiece of ornate silver on a long chain of polished silver. "Miss Holmes," he said, "your mission is a simple one. Simply give this watch to Major Petrie. He will place information about the Confederate army inside a secret chamber in the watch and return it to you. Then, simply bring the pocket watch back to me and I'll deliver the information to the Secretary of War, Mr. Stanton . . ." Dr. Gleason paused briefly, ". . . Miss Holmes, are you still willing to spy for our nation?"

There was no hesitation on my part—if Mrs. Greenhow could engage in espionage for her beloved Confederacy then I, too, could spy for my beloved Union. I looked Dr. Gleason squarely in the eye when I gave my answer, "I'll ask my driver to prepare my carriage at once . . ."

"No," Dr. Gleason almost shouted, "you can't leave Washington by carriage. You might be searched again."

"Why should that matter?" I asked. "If searched, nothing would be found on me except a watch with a hollow chamber. And surely if I explained my mission to the bridge guards . . ."

Dr. Gleason rose to his feet and looked—no, he glared down at me. His voice conveyed impatience when he said, "I have already explained that you must pose as a Confederate, so you must travel as a Confederate would travel to Richmond—not in your carriage on open roads, but under the cover of darkness on back roads and in smugglers' boats. I will escort you on the first part of your journey to the farmhouse of a gentleman named Mr. Jones . . . Can you prepare at once?"

In answer, I summoned Bessie and we went upstairs to pack a valise. While we sorted through my gowns I was careful not to select dresses adorned with patriotic ribbons or pins. Within the hour I was bidding Bessie good-bye; she has a simple, trusting soul for she readily believed my story that Dr. Gleason had recommended that I visit a health sanitarium for a much needed rest.

CHAPTER FIVE

As Dr. Gleason helped me into his small carriage he asked if I wore the silver brooch he had given me. Because of my pride as a Unionist, it disturbed me to wear a piece of jewelry that symbolized the Confederate States of America, but I nodded and showed him the brooch pinned to my collar. In a firm voice he reminded me, "Remember. The very moment you meet Major Petrie, show him the brooch."

Dr. Gleason snapped the reins as we drove through the crowded streets, and soon the lights of the city were behind us. For several hours we sped through the farmlands of Maryland; we rode in almost complete silence since it was difficult to speak over the clopping sounds of the horse's hooves. At times Dr. Gleason pulled his carriage to the side of the road to rest his horse, and then we spoke about the customs of Southern ladies so as to perfect my portrayal of a Southerner (fortunately I had inherited my mother's soft Southern drawl, so my accent would not sound foreign to a Virginian's ear).

During our final roadside stop, Dr. Gleason examined his horse's right hoof; a small stone was wedged in its shoe and I held a lantern above him while he took a knife and dug out the pebble. As he tended to the horse, a patrol of Federals came upon us and demanded to know our business at that hour of night. Before we gave an answer, one of the soldiers spotted Dr. Gleason's medical bag on the seat of his carriage and called out, "This here gent is a doctor. Let's move on."

As we climbed back into the carriage Dr. Gleason laughed that unattractive laugh of his. "Miss Holmes, he said, "I have discovered that a medical bag is as good as a passport. No one ever suspects a doctor of wrong doing."

His laughter echoed in my thoughts for the next hour, as I puzzled over the meaning of his words that a doctor is never suspected. Suspected of what? I kept his troubling words in mind as we entered a thick patch of woods and crossed over a shallow stream before turning up a steep bluff towards a house with darkened windows.

CHAPTER SIX

Dr. Gleason guided his horse into a shed that leaned against the house before taking my arm and leading me towards a back door. His knock was answered at once by a thin man dressed in a nightshirt; he held a candle above his head which cast shadows over his bearded face. In a sleepy voice he mumbled, "Dr. Gleason? We weren't expecting you until tomorrow. Mr. Jones won't be home until daybreak."

Dr. Gleason's reply was quick, "This is Miss Holmes, Henry . . . she is willing to wait until tomorrow. Has her passage across the Potomac been arranged?"

"Mr. Jones, himself, will ferry her across." The man yawned as he beckoned us to follow him into a parlor that was dimly lit by a low-burning fire in the hearth. In the faint light Dr. Gleason's face was unrecognizable and yet, even in the shadowy darkness at the front door, he was easily recognized and greeted with familiarity.

We were brought cups of tea and a basket of buttered bread and we ate in complete silence as though the darkness of the room forbade talk. Afterwards, Henry brought in my valise and showed me to an adjoining room where I could rest.

At the door Dr. Gleason asked if I carried any money that would identify me as a Unionist and I gave him my coin purse for safekeeping. In return he gave me one American dollar bill and a thick envelope filled with Confederate money. He whispered, "The American dollar is for Mr. Jones who will ask you for payment when he ferries you across the river. Use the Confederate dollars for food—and bribes. If you are arrested as a spy, use the money to purchase your freedom—there are always corrupt men who will look the other way if they are paid handsomely."

He then gave me a brown paper stamped, Travel Pass, and explained, "Miss Holmes, this pass allows freedom of travel inside the Confederacy. If you should lose it, you can buy another pass by giving a bribe of $100 to a government official." Dr. Gleason then bade me farewell and good luck and after he had left for Washington I closeted myself inside the small room.

Snuffing out the candle I sat in the dark by the window. Thoughts cluttered my mind and sleep escaped me as I watched the clouds of night sliding past the yellow moon. Perhaps an hour had lapsed when a horse and rider trotted around the house and passed in front of my window. The horseman was wrapped in a long cloak; he looked much like a shadow of the night. He dismounted slowly and walked his horse towards the shed and moments later I heard the shutting of a heavy door. Gathering up my skirts, I crept over to the door and inched it open.

Two men were speaking in lowered voices. The first voice I recognized at once as the voice of Dr. Gleason—he had lied to me! He hadn't returned to

Washington after all! I heard him say, "Treat Miss Holmes well. She will prove invaluable to the Confederacy . . . her beauty will open any door."

The other man muttered something in a raspy voice and Dr. Gleason laughed his hideous laugh before saying, "Miss Holmes' innocence equals her beauty . . . her trust in me was obvious, so it was a simple matter to enlist her as a spy . . . as long as we can dupe her into believing she serves the Union, the Confederacy can use her as a courier." He laughed again and though his voice was low I clearly heard him say, "No, she doesn't realize what she's carrying for us . . ."

A heavy door opened and closed again and I rushed back to the window and lifted a corner of the drapes. Minutes later Dr. Gleason's carriage rounded the corner of the house; under the moon's light I glimpsed his face. His face was the face of a Confederate sympathizer. His face was the face of a traitor!

I trembled with anger. Anger at him for deceiving me. And anger at myself for being duped so easily. I recalled his words—*a doctor is never suspected*—indeed I had trusted him simply because he was a physician.

And then I recalled his other words, *she doesn't realize what she is carrying*—surely Dr. Gleason referred to the pocket watch. I remembered then, the derision in his voice when he stressed that I must travel like a Confederate to avoid being searched at a bridge leaving Washington. That could only mean one thing: the secret chamber in the pocket watch wasn't empty, after all.

CHAPTER SEVEN

Quietly, I turned the key in the lock and fully closed the drapes before brightening the lamp. Then, sitting at the desk, I took the watch from my pocket.

Using great care I turned the watch over and over looking for a piece that might slide open to reveal the secret chamber. I pulled on the chain and tapped on the face of the watch, and my persistence soon won out; upon twisting the stem of the watch, the back panel popped open and a narrow strip of onionskin paper fluttered out.

Biting at my lower lip I unfolded the paper. It was a message, but it was written in a jumble of letters. It read:

OEENGNNCP YKNN JGUKVCVG VQ CVVCEM
LQJPUVQP'U CTOA KH JG DGNKGXGU JG KU
QWVPWODGTGF. UGPF HCNUG OGUUCIGU VQ
YCUJKPVQP VJCV FQWDNGU VJG UKBG QH
QWT CTOA.

I stared at the hodgepodge of letters and tried to make sense of them, but obviously the message was written in a secret language of code. Carefully, I refolded the message and placed it back in the chamber before shutting the back panel. Then, sitting at the window, I parted the drapes and stared out into the night, as anger and fear swelled up inside of me.

Chapter Eight

By the time the sun showed itself in the sky I had decided what I should do. It was clear that Dr. Gleason meant to dupe me into believing I would serve as a courier spy for the Union, when in fact I would carry coded messages for the Confederacy. I would do as that villain wanted and go to Richmond, but I would not give Major Petrie the message in the watch—I would destroy the message and convince him somehow that I never knew of its existence. If Major Petrie should believe my story, he would give me another message as planned, and I would return by a different route to Washington and deliver the watch to the War Department—and I would report Dr. Gleason's treasonous act to Mr. Lincoln, himself.

As I sat there I mulled over one problem: how could I dispose of the message in the watch before I met Major Petrie, but at the same time avoid making him suspicious that I had guessed their true purpose for me?

My thoughts were interrupted by a talkative servant girl named Millie. As she laid out my breakfast she told me that Mr. Jones had arrived home earlier that morning (he must have been the man Dr. Gleason had spoken to). And she confided that her master left word not to be disturbed, because he intended to sleep until dusk—at that hour he would ferry me across the river.

For much of that morning I wandered around the lawns of the house. At times I lost my courage and toyed with the idea of fleeing down the road until I found a Union patrol. Common sense won out though, for the servant girl had mentioned that Mr. Jones's farm was large, nearly 540 acres in all, so if I took flight he could easily track me down before I escaped his property.

For much of that afternoon I sat looking out a window; the house sat on a high bluff about a hundred feet above the waters of the Potomac River. It was a magnificent view; from that great height I could see for miles on either side of the river and in the distance I could see Virginia on the Confederate side of the Potomac. Throughout those hours Union boats patrolled the waters that touched the Maryland side of the river. At one point my courage faded again and I waved wildly at one of the patrol boats, but the soldiers misunderstood and whistled and waved back at me. I chided myself for acting cowardly and new determination to help my nation lent me fresh fortitude to wait patiently for dusk.

*****

Dusk came too soon. Just as I finished eating, Millie came into the parlor and picking up my valise she asked me to follow her. I slipped into my coat and walked down the hill behind her.

The scent of night was on the earth; billows of grey fog rolled over the darkening waters and edged over the rocks where I was instructed to wait for Mr. Jones. The land in the near distance was not yet clouded with fog and I watched as a man, dressed in a long cloak, walked down the hill towards a scraggle of bushes.

He gestured at me to join him and when I stood before him my heart pounded so loudly that I feared he would hear and know my fear.

He appeared an ordinary man of ordinary build, but it was impossible to see if his face was ordinary, because his features were concealed by the folds of his cloak. In a muffled voice he said, "Stranger, do you wish to cross the river?"

I nodded, thinking how peculiar that he would act as though he were unaware of my presence in his house or my need to cross the Potomac.

He asked, "Are you willing to pay my $1 fee?"

How clever of him! If questioned by the authorities I would have to admit that I paid him and that he addressed me as a traveler and stranger. I gave the American dollar to Mr. Jones and he tucked it into his boot before moving aside to reveal a rowboat hidden in the bushes. Ignoring his hand, I stepped into the bow of the boat.

Mr. Jones climbed into the stern of the flat-bottomed boat, but even as he picked up the oars he hesitated and I followed his gaze towards a nearby house where a black cloth hung from a second floor window. Mr. Jones caught my eye and whispered, "Shh, stranger."

A moment later a Union boat drifted by; in its bow sat four soldiers armed with rifles. The coward in me nearly called out for help, but the fog swallowed them up as though they had never existed. I knew then that they would never have heard me—surely Mr. Jones would have taken his oar and clubbed me to death. So, I sat in silence and stared up at the window with the black cloth and when it was removed Mr. Jones dipped his oars into the water and we slid away from the bushes.

While he rowed, he whistled—a shrill, unpleasant whistle that sounded like the whistling of wind through graveyard stones. I wanted to ask him to keep quiet, for the darkness and the icy splash of water and the haunting sound of his whistle frightened me. I feared I was being rowed towards my grave.

*****

After what seemed like an eternity, the boat glided into a cove on the Virginian side of the Potomac. Bunching the cloak around his face, Mr. Jones stood up to hail a coarse-looking youth who led me towards another, much larger, boat and soon I was steaming towards the Confederate's capital city.

By the time the lights of Richmond were in sight, I felt bone weary. Indeed, throughout those long hours, I never slept, for my stomach was pitted with pains of hunger. And fear.

CHAPTER NINE

The pier in Richmond was littered with foul smelling rubbish crawling with worms and buzzing flies. I placed my valise near a piling on which a fat sea gull roosted and hired a ragged boy to find me a carriage.

The child was quick in finding me a driver and I rewarded him with another coin which he clenched tightly in his dirty hand.

As I was driven through the streets of Richmond it seemed as if I were in another city, for the Richmond I saw that morning was unfamiliar to me. Gone were the quiet, lovely streets I remembered and in their place were noise-filled streets lined with saloons with swinging doors through which drunkards stumbled. Faro houses—parlors where men gambled on dice and cards—were squeezed in between shabby houses with high windows where women with painted faces waved at the sailors and soldiers staggering by. For once I was glad Mother wasn't with me, for she would have wept to see her beloved Richmond soiled by the dirt of War.

At last my carriage turned onto a street that was dear to me—each house and tree and lamppost brought back precious memories as my carriage drew up in front of the house in which my mother had been born and raised.

It was an elegant house of brick, three stories tall, with ivy encircling the chimneys that stood at either end. As I pushed open the iron gate and climbed the wide steps to the porch another flood of memories washed over me. Memories of family gatherings on summer evenings: of Father pouring pink lemonade and Mother sitting on the porch swing with needlework in her hands, of Julia playing her flute and all of us singing and laughing. There was always an abundance of laughter in those days. A few years ago when my parents died in that terrible train crash in Virginia my sister and I returned to Mother's home in Richmond and there we found solace from our grief.

I thought of all that as I turned the key in the lock. How I dreaded entering the house, for it would be cold and empty.

My house was not empty, after all. A tiny, round-faced child of perhaps two years of age, sat on the bottom step of the staircase. Golden hair tumbled about her face and her eyes were large circles of the softest blue. When she saw me she pushed clumsily off the step and toddling down the hall she cried out for her mother. Quietly, I closed the front door and followed the child.

In the parlor I came upon the little girl in the arms of her mother. The woman was older than I, perhaps nineteen or twenty years, but the grey that streaked her twist of black hair and the shadows beneath her brown eyes gave her the appearance of a much older woman. Her complexion, though, was lovely and youthful. She quieted the child with kisses and coming towards me she asked, "Who are you? What are you doing in my home?"

I was so flabbergasted that she questioned my presence in my own home that I stammered, "My name is Louisa Holmes . . . this is my house. What are you doing here?"

Her brow was marked with faint lines as though she frowned often and without responding to my question, she went over to the desk, took out a document and handed it to me. It was a lease for the rental of the house for two years—and it was signed by my family's solicitor. I read the brief document, noting that the woman and her husband, Mr. Peter Beecham, had paid handsomely for the use of my home.

Handing the paper back to her I began to say, "My solicitor neglected to mention that he had leased my house to—" when the smell of burning food came to us. Snatching up her daughter Mrs. Beecham fled towards the kitchen.

I placed my valise behind the parlor door and sat down in a chair beside the piano. As I waited for Mrs. Beecham's return I looked around the room. Nothing had changed in the past two years; the velvet couches looked as comfortable as always; the china figurines stood in their usual places on the shelves; and the picture Mother had painted of Virginia's mountains stood on the easel between the windows. Everything was as before—warm and inviting and spotlessly clean. I saw, then, that there was a change. A small change, but one that chilled my very soul—above the fireplace mantle hung a Confederate sword.

CHAPTER TEN

Oddly the presence of that sword made me feel like a trespasser in my own home. Perhaps that explains why I didn't reveal my presence when a man came into the parlor reading a newspaper. He didn't notice me sitting in the far corner, so I took advantage of my unknown presence to study him.

He was, I decided, a gentleman that most ladies would never label as sophisticated, for he wore no beard or sideburns and his clothes were wrinkled as though he had worn them for days. Indeed his face wore an expression of absolute weariness and it was then that I noticed he carried a physician's bag.

His weariness didn't age him though, for he looked youthful, perhaps nineteen years of age. He wasn't especially tall, but neither was he short; and although he wasn't heavy of bone, he wasn't thin. Oh, he defied description, for he was a person of contradictions. His hair was brown and yet streaked with blond—or was his hair blond and streaked with brown? His nose was strong, but not overlarge, for the cut of his cheek-bones and chin was wide. And yet, despite the strength of his face, he had the appearance of a kind man, a gentle man.

His eyes were lowered as he read the newspaper, and I wondered if they were the same soft blue as his daughter's eyes, since in all probability he was Mr. Peter Beecham.

As I watched him, his expression changed, for whatever he was reading interested him deeply. First, he appeared disturbed by what he read, but then a broad smile invaded his face and he tossed the news-paper onto a table and hurried from the room.

Curious what had caused him so much pleasure, I picked up the newspaper and read,

General George McClellan is landing 100,000 sol-diers of his Army of the Potomac. Even now, Fed-eral tents and campfires stretch across the entire width of Virginia's Peninsula. It is believed that General McClellan will march on Richmond . . .

How strange that a Confederate would smile when he read that an enemy army threatened his city with invasion. How very strange, indeed.

CHAPTER ELEVEN

A short while later Mrs. Beecham came into the parlor holding her daughter's hand; the little girl hid shyly behind her mother's skirts. Mrs. Beecham seemed surprised that I had waited for her, so before she spoke, I did. "Mrs. Beecham," I began, "as far as I am concerned your lease is valid, but I have business to attend to while I'm in Richmond. Would you mind if I roomed here, as a paying boarder of course, until my return to Raleigh (I realized it would be wiser to pretend I was from another Southern city).

Mrs. Beecham smiled. "Of course you shall stay here, Miss Holmes. There is nowhere else you could stay since there are no vacancies in the hotels or boarding houses of Richmond; this city overflows because hundreds of men arrive daily to enlist as soldiers." Her smile deepened as she added most graciously, "Please stay as my guest, not as my boarder, for truly this is your home . . . I would feel wicked turning you out."

I thanked her and asked, "Will your husband mind my intrusion?"

My question brought a curious change to her face. Her brow and her eyes and her mouth tightened as though she had been shrunk by the sun; she seemed to age several years in mere seconds. In a peculiar voice she said, "My husband is dead. He died last summer during the Battle of Manassas . . ." She turned her eyes towards the sword hanging above the mantle and in that queer voice she murmured, "I blame Abraham Lincoln for my husband's death. If I were a man I'd kill him and each and every Unionist."

The venom in her voice frightened me, for I knew if she discovered that I was a Unionist, she would turn that hatred against me. Then, almost at once, the anger discoloring her face faded, because she noticed the silver brooch on my collar that marked me as a loyal Confederate. Her mood changed in that instant and smiling sweetly she beckoned me to follow her upstairs to the third floor. As I picked up my valise I glanced over at her smiling face and thought how bizarre that her temperament could change so rapidly, like the rapid color changes of that odd little creature, the chameleon lizard.

*****

Mrs. Beecham led me to a bedroom that I knew well; during my family's holidays in Richmond, the room had always served as my sister's chamber. Apparently, Mrs. Beecham and her daughter were lodging in my old bedroom, but I said nothing in complaint.

I put my valise under the corner desk before drawing back the drapes. Sunlight drenched the room and I looked around, comforted by the familiarity of my surroundings. My sister's flute and music books were lying on a shelf, her bed was still draped with the lace comforter our grandmother had crocheted, and a bottle of Julia's favorite perfume stood on the silver tray that bore her initials. The large windows, the soft rug beside the bed, and the oak dresser with its many drawers were all so familiar to me and yet I still felt like a stranger, as though I had no right to be there in my own home.

Mrs. Beecham brought me a pitcher of cool water and a towel and after she closed the door behind her I unfastened my traveling dress. Clad only in my drawers and hoops I poured water into a basin and washed my face and neck. The water refreshed me, for the long journey had left me feeling soiled.

As I washed my arms I wished I could be done with the curious business of spying and could return to Washington, but I had to wait for Major Petrie to call on me. How I dreaded that meeting—I still hadn't decided how to destroy the message in the watch without bringing suspicion on myself—after all, supposedly I didn't know the message even existed, so I couldn't remove it—the message had to remain in the watch, but yet it mustn't be read by the Confederates. As I dried my hands with the towel my gaze fell on the basin of water and I knew the solution to my dilemma.

Taking the silver watch from my pocket I twisted the stem and the back panel popped open. Carefully, I removed the paper and then copied the message, letter by letter, into my journal. Once that was completed, I dipped my finger into the basin and dripped water over the strip of paper until the black ink smeared, until the message of letters was unreadable. Once the paper had dried, I resealed it within the secret chamber of the watch.

Under the copy of the message in my journal I wrote a detailed description of both traitors, Dr. Gleason and Mr. Jones, before turning to another page to write,

Drawing by Joy Renee Maine

30 March, 1862.

I have ruined the message in the watch, so I am now prepared to meet Major Robert Petrie. He will be angry, no doubt, when he discovers the message from Dr. Gleason is unreadable, but I have thought up a fiction that should convince him of my innocence in the matter.

CHAPTER TWELVE

Later that night Mrs. Beecham knocked at my chamber door and invited me to join her for supper. I was terribly hungry, so I accepted her kind invitation.

The dining room was dimly lit by a gas lamp on the sideboard; the room had been rearranged to allow space for a little table and chair at which sat the child. Her name was Ashley and when she saw me she lowered her head, though she lifted her blue eyes to peek at me.

Just as I had taken my seat a gentleman, the physician I had spied upon earlier that day, hurried into the room. When he saw me he stood quite still and then he bowed his head, his eyes on mine.

I offered him my hand as Mrs. Beecham made the introductions; he was her brother, Dr. Hugh Ryle, and he, too, lodged in the house. Mrs. Beecham explained who I was and that I would be staying for awhile, but when she mentioned that I had just arrived from Raleigh Dr. Ryle looked at me with the oddest expression—

I had the distinct impression that he saw me for who I was—a pretender, a fake, a spy. I felt myself stiffen, for I fully expected him to ask questions that would reveal me as a Northerner.

My discomfort quickly faded, however, because Dr. Ryle asked me nothing personal; indeed, he only spoke about the child Ashley, or the unseasonably wet weather, or his work at the hospital. And so, as he spoke, the disquiet disappeared from my heart, for his voice carried no threat, no hint that he suspected me of wrongdoing. His voice. How could I ever describe his voice. It was a most pleasant voice, traced with the accent of Virginia, deep and rich and low. And peaceful. His voice was utterly peaceful, the voice of a man of compassion.

He and his sister addressed me as Miss Holmes and I protested their formality and asked that they call me by my Christian name and, in turn, they asked that I call them Charleen and Hugh.

Charleen passed me a dish of stew. At least it had the appearance of stew since there were slices of carrot and potato in a floury gravy; however, it tasted like wallpaper paste because it lacked spices and meat. As though Charleen had read my thoughts she asked, "Can you still find meat in the butcher shops of Raleigh?"

I didn't know of course, for I had never been to Raleigh, but I reasoned that all Southern cities lacked food, so I shook my head no and tried to swallow the awful stuff without choking.

Charleen's eyes narrowed and stabbing a potato with her fork she said, "Mr. Lincoln is a baboon. He knew when he blocked our seaports that we ladies of the South couldn't receive foods from Europe . . . he knew that we would be forced to prepare suppers that should be slop for pigs."

Smiling, Hugh said, "Charleen, I doubt Mr. Lincoln is intentionally trying to make our diet bland.

His blockade has one purpose—to prevent supplies from reaching the Confederacy's armies. Mr. Lincoln's clever strategy may shorten this War."

Charleen's face became rigid with anger. In a bitter voice she retorted, "I am tired, brother, of hearing you defend Mr. Lincoln. You are in danger of becoming a Unionist."

Brother and sister stared across the table at each other and I felt uncomfortably intrusive, for it was obvious that the War was a sore subject between them. At that very moment, Ashley fell off her chair and although she didn't appear hurt, she cried pitifully as though she had broken every tiny bone. Strangely, it was her uncle who rescued and comforted her. At first Charleen remained sitting as though she hadn't heard Ashley, but then she gathered up her daughter and took her upstairs.

When we were alone, Hugh said, "I must apologize, Louisa. My sister and I have different views about the War. She has become . . . sensitive . . . since the death of her husband at Manassas."

"There's no need to apologize," I murmured. "I, too, lost someone dear to me at the Battle of Bull Run . . . my fiancé, Adam Sorenson."

Hugh lifted one eyebrow. "Bull Run? In the South, that battle is remembered as the Battle of Manassas . . . to call it by any other name could prove dangerous. Take care what you say, Louisa. Careless words could mark you as a Unionist."

I put down my fork and mumbling that I wasn't hungry, I fled upstairs before he asked what a Unionist was doing in Richmond.

*****

That first night back in Richmond was a sleepless one, for my thoughts denied me sleep. I thought about Major Petrie and rehearsed what I would say to him. I thought about Charleen's strange and sudden mood changes. And I thought about her brother, Hugh, and wondered why he had warned me to speak with care instead of calling for my arrest.

I passed the hours of my second day watching Confederate officers walk past my window with hope that one of them would pause and knock at the door, but Major Petrie never called. That night Charleen, Ashley and I ate another supper of pasty stew. The conversation was cordial, for Hugh was at the hospital and I purposely avoided any mention of the War.

My second night of rest was disturbed by a frightening dream—I dreamt that Charleen unveiled me as a spy and vented her rage against me. Unable to sleep, I rose early and spent the morning hours pacing the floor of the parlor waiting for Major Petrie. After the noon hour my impatience bested me and putting on my cloak I went out into the streets of the city.

*****

I walked without direction, but as I walked I began to realize that I needn't waste my time waiting for the major—if I spotted an important general or a Confederate congressman or some new weapon I could report that discovery upon my return to Washington. I was nearly tricked into acting as an agent of espionage for the Confederacy by unscrupulous men, therefore, why not act as an agent for the Union.

Thankfully my memory is keen, for I would have drawn suspicion if I had carried my journal and recorded my observations in public. Instead I decided that I could memorize every little thing of importance, and later, in the privacy of my chamber, I could write those observations in my journal.

The first person of importance that I chose to observe was President Jefferson Davis and it was a simple matter to learn that he lived on Church Street, a lovely street that I knew well. A short walk later I found myself standing outside the Davis mansion, a formal house of white walls and graceful pillars.

Pausing outside the gates, I pretended to fuss with the buttons of my gloves when the front door swung open. From the corner of my eye I watched a tall, gaunt-looking man dressed all in black—black trousers, coat and hat—he looked like an undertaker instead of a president, for that gentleman was none other than Jeff Davis. As I watched, he mounted a fine-looking horse and trotted through his gates and down the street.

I was so intent on watching him that I didn't notice a gentleman had come up behind me. "Good afternoon," he said, and startled, I spun around and looked up into the smiling eyes of Hugh Ryle.

"What do you think of the president of the Confederacy?" he asked me and I answered truthfully, "I know very little about him."

"Then I will tell you what I know about Jefferson Davis," Hugh smiled as he took my arm and led me across the street towards a carriage. "A few weeks ago, on February 22—the very birthday of George Washington—Jefferson Davis stood beneath the city's statue of Washington and took the oath as president of the Confederate States of America. Rain poured down on my head and the heads of thousands who had gathered for the ceremony. As I stood in that cold rain and watched Davis standing in the shadow of that statue I knew he was comparing himself as the leader of rebellious states to George Washington, the leader of rebellious colonies. The obvious comparison angered me, Louisa, for unlike George Washington, Jeff Davis is a traitor."

I caught my breath and whispered, "Are you a Unionist as your sister claimed?"

"I am. And if my sister mentions that fact to the wrong person I will be arrested—just as you will be arrested, Louisa, if you are found out as the spy you are."

My heart thumped wildly. "Hugh, why do you label me a spy?"

"Because I believe you are a spy," he answered simply. "A few years ago I studied medicine in Washington, D.C. While there I once heard your father speak eloquently of his loyalty to the Union. I assume you share your father's loyalty, and I assume, too, that you did not arrive here from Raleigh, but from Washington, D.C."

There was no use denying the truth, so instead I asked, "Hugh, if you are a Unionist, why do you stay here in Richmond?"

Sorrow underlined his voice when he said, "I have my reasons for staying," but in a stronger tone he added, "perhaps it would be wise if you returned to Washington, Louisa, before my sister uncovers your secret . . . Charleen is fiercely loyal to the Confederacy. She would consider it her sacred duty to have you arrested."

His concern touched me, but in an equally strong voice I said, "Hugh, I, too, have reasons for staying in Richmond."

He looked at me as though trying to read into my heart and soul and mind before saying, "If you won't heed my advice to leave this city I will show you the consequences of what could happen." And taking my arm he helped me into his carriage and drove us to Franklin Street where he parked near a building that my father had once shown me—it was a small building where slave dealers once penned up Negro men, women and children before displaying them on blocks at slave auctions. Puzzled, I asked, "Why did you bring me here, Hugh?"

He stared at the barred windows of the building as he said, "During his inaugural speech Jefferson Davis criticized the Union for filling up Northern prisons with "civil officers, peaceful citizens . . . and gentle women." Davis accused Abe Lincoln of arresting citizens without civil process, of suspending the writ of habeas corpus and of imprisoning men and women who merely stated their opinions.

"And yet, Louisa, within weeks after Davis's inauguration, a bill was passed by both houses of the Confederate Congress which gave him the power to suspend the right of habeas corpus.

"Then, on the first day of this month he placed the entire city of Richmond under martial law and he empowered a dim-witted man named General Winder to arrest anyone suspected of disloyalty to the Confederacy. Two of my oldest friends—Mr. Franklin Stearns, the distiller of whiskey, and Reverend Alden Bosserman—were among those who were arrested.

"Franklin was arrested at his estate, Tree Hill. His crime: he spoke in support of the Union. And Reverend Bosserman's crime was considered even more serious: he prayed for Union victory."

"A minister was arrested for praying?" I asked in disbelief.

Hugh nodded. "Reverend Bosserman asked his congregation to pray that "this unholy rebellion be crushed out." Supposedly that prayer was the final proof of his disloyalty to the Confederacy and thus he was arrested."

I looked at the slave pen. "Hugh, are your friends inside these walls? Is this terrible place a prison for disloyal citizens?"

He nodded, his eyes creased as though with pain when he said, "This place of suffering is called Castle Godwin. Over 200 men and women are crushed into twelve rooms—they drink from filthy buckets of water, they eat food that is soiled by the droppings of rats, and they sleep on pallets that are crawling with lice. Their crimes: careless words spoken against Jeff Davis and his rebels."

Hugh snapped the reins and as we drove away from the prison he said, "Two of the prisoners in Castle Godwin are Union spies—a gentleman named Timothy Webster and a lady named Mrs. Hattie Lawton. If you choose to stay in Richmond, Louisa, you risk discovery as a spy. You risk imprisonment in Castle Godwin."

CHAPTER THIRTEEN

That same night, near the hour of midnight, I was awoken by crying. Ashley's cries began as low sobs, but soon changed into frightened screams. Slipping into my robe I ran out into the hall and knocked on Charleen's door just as Hugh came running up the stairs. I stepped aside as he pushed open her door, but I followed him into the room.

Ashley was sitting in the corner of her crib; her face awash with tears. When she saw her uncle she reached her hands towards him and he picked her up and cradled her in his arms.

The room was dimly lit, so at first I didn't see Charleen sitting at the dressing table. Then I saw more clearly and horror crept into my soul. Charleen was dressed in a long, white gown with a veil of lace floating down her back. She sat like a marble statue, staring at her reflection in the looking glass; her face had the appearance of a mask, for she had powdered her skin a chalky white and had painted her cheeks and lips with globs of red rouge.

Hugh handed Ashley to me; she no longer cried, but she trembled as though she knew, in spite of her tender years, that something was terribly wrong with her mother. I stepped into the shadows so that Ashley couldn't see her mother's face, but I watched as Hugh knelt beside his sister. Only then did Charleen seem to notice him; smiling, she murmured, "Brother dear, is it time to leave for the church . . . is Peter there, waiting for me?"

Hugh took his sister's hands in his. "Charleen," he said in a soothing voice, "Peter's been delayed. Your wedding day must wait."

The smile on Charleen's face fell away, but she allowed her brother to lead her over to the bed where she laid down without argument. He covered her with a quilt, and even as she closed her eyes she smiled and said, "Tell Peter I shall count the seconds until we speak our vows."

Hugh gestured at me to follow him down the hall to my own room. There he shut the door and I sat in the rocker with Ashley. She still trembled, but she seemed content to stay in my arms.

For a while we sat in silence as though neither of us wished to speak of Charleen. In the silence Ashley's eyes fluttered close as she drifted into sleep. Hugh brushed the child's golden hair from her eyes and in a lowered voice he said, "Louisa, yesterday you asked me why I, a Unionist, would stay in Richmond . . . you now know the reason . . . my sister is ill."

There was another brief silence before he spoke for a long while as though he had to rid himself of troubling words. He said, "Three years ago my sister married her childhood sweetheart . . . Peter Beecham was a good and honest man. He was devoted to Charleen and later to their daughter. When War came Peter and Charleen were caught up in the romance of war . . . he enlisted immediately and rode off to battle like a knight in shining armor . . . my sister sent him off happily . . . she believed he would return victorious and unscathed like a heroic figure in a medieval tale.

"Last summer, during the Battle of Manassas, Peter was beheaded by a cannonball. He was buried on the battlefield . . . one of his fellow officers brought back Peter's sword and presented it to Charleen. For months my sister drifted around this house like a ghost. She barely ate or spoke . . . she wept constantly . . . then one night she came downstairs dressed in her wedding gown and asked me to drive her to the church . . . she believed that Peter was waiting there to marry her. I hoped that episode of insanity would not be repeated, but it has been repeated. Often. Too often my sister slips into another world where her husband is still alive. Perhaps that other world offers Charleen some peace from our own war-torn world. Perhaps when this War ends, my sister won't have reason to escape into that other world."

Hugh glanced down at Ashley; she slept peacefully in my arms. In a bewildered voice he said, "Oddly, it is the simple act of sleeping that returns Charleen to normal. Tomorrow morning when she awakes she may wonder why she is dressed in her wedding gown, but she'll remember nothing of what happened tonight."

He looked then at me. "Louisa, I have confided in you. Can't you find the courage to confide in me . . . why did you come to Richmond?"

Chapter Fourteen

Hugh's eyes were of the softest blue, or was it the gentleness in their expression that lent softness to the color. I looked into those gentle eyes and my heart whispered that I should trust him. Slowly I stood up so as not to awaken Ashley and placing her on the bed I covered her with a blanket. Then, going over to the wardrobe, I took the journal and pocket watch from their hiding place.

First, I told him about Dr. Gleason and Major Petrie before opening the back of the watch to show him the smeared strip of paper. I then showed him the copy of the message in my journal and he puzzled over the meaning of the letters before suddenly leaving the room. He returned a short time later carrying his doctor's bag and from it he withdrew an object: a flattened disc of bronze. On the disc there were two circles of the alphabet's letters; one circle around the outer edge and another circle of letters around the center of the disc.

Hugh said, "A few weeks ago I had a patient—a fellow who worked in the espionage department here in Richmond—he was foolish enough to trust me. He showed me this disc and explained how the Confederates use discs to write and decipher coded messages. After his death I kept the disc hoping it would prove useful one day."

I begged him to show me how the disc worked and he explained thusly. He said, "The inner circle of the alphabet spins . . . to break the code we need to know which letter in the inner circle to move under the letter A in the outer circle. Then the rest of the letters are paired up and we can decipher the code."

To better explain, Hugh spun the inner circle until the letter B fell under the letter A. "For example, Louisa, the word c-a-b would be coded as d-b-c."

Understanding came to me even as I realized that unless we knew the key letter of the code, we wouldn't be able to decipher the message.

Hugh was optimistic that we could uncover the key letter. He asked, "Did Dr. Gleason instruct you to say some particular word or phrase to Major Petrie? Perhaps the letter would be revealed in that word?"

I thought for a moment. "I wasn't told to say anything in particular. He did emphasize one thing though . . . to show Major Petrie a patriotic brooch so that he would recognize me as the courier. The brooch!" I nearly shouted. Rushing over to the wardrobe I unpinned the brooch from the collar of a dress and gave it to Hugh. He stared at the letter C carved into the silver and his smile matched my own.

Hugh spun the C on the inner circle until it rested under the A on the outer circle of the disc and within minutes we had unraveled the jumble of letters,

OEENGNNCP YKNN JGUKVCVG VQ CVVCEM

LQJPUVQP'U CTOA KH JG DGNKGXGU JG KU

QWVPWODGTGF. UGPF HCNUG OGUUCIGU VQ
YCUJKPIVQP VJCV FQWDNG VJG UKBG QH
QWT CTOA.

to read:

MCCLELLAN WILL HESITATE TO ATTACK
JOHNSTON'S ARMY IF HE BELIEVES HE IS
OUTNUMBERED. SEND FALSE MESSAGES TO
WASHINGTON THAT DOUBLE THE SIZE OF
OUR ARMY.

"Could it be true that McClellan would hesitate if he thought he was outnumbered?" Hugh asked.

"Perhaps," I smiled. "General McClellan has a reputation for not taking chances. I daresay he'd still be marching his army in parades around Washington if President Lincoln hadn't issued an Order for battle."

Midnight had long passed; truly Hugh looked weary from his long hours at the hospital, so after he checked on his sister (she was sleeping peacefully) he bade me good night and went downstairs to his room.

Before dimming my lamp, I wrote all that Hugh had told me in my journal. Often, I looked over at Ashley; her circle face and her golden hair lent her the appearance of a fragile angel. As I looked upon that sleeping angel I thought how cruel war is—war took her father and sickened her mother—how sad that even tiny angels are touched by war.

CHAPTER FIFTEEN

The next morning I found a bundle of napkins outside my door (Hugh must have left them there) and after I had changed Ashley's wet napkins, I carried her downstairs to the kitchen. There was only stale bread in the cupboard and so I soaked a slice of bread with warm milk and mashed it up. Ashley ate hungrily while I sat near her and drank coffee.

Some time later Hugh came into the kitchen and while I poured him a cup of coffee he said in a lowered voice, "I have some hopeful news. A friend . . . a fellow Unionist . . . stopped by early this morning to tell me that the Federal army broke camp yesterday morning. General McClellan has begun his march up the Peninsula."

Struggling to keep my own voice low in spite of my excitement I asked, "How long do you think it will take for the Federals to reach Richmond?"

He paused before saying, "I'm uncertain. The rains this spring have been so heavy that the Peninsula is like a sea of mud." He put down his cup and leaned closer. "Years ago I went hunting on the Peninsula . . . it was the spring time and the dark woods and the few roads were deep with mud. It took all my strength to walk because I had to wrench my feet from the mud . . . it was exhausting work . . . it took me an hour to walk one mile. Supposedly, the soldiers are finding their march through the mud just as exhausting. My Unionist friend said the Peninsula is littered with shoes and coats and blankets . . . any item of weight too burdensome to carry has been cast off into the mud and—"

Hugh didn't finish his sentence for Charleen came through the door; she was dressed in an ordinary gown and her face was scrubbed clean and I knew, somehow, that she was herself again. She seemed cheerful enough until she opened the cupboard and discovered it bare. "Brother dear," she sighed, "we are in dire need of food. Have you any money?" Hugh handed her several dollars and smiling at me she said, "Louisa, I despise the robber prices that must be paid for food. I refuse to pay $1.50 for a pound of coffee, so I shall make coffee out of roasted acorns and bacon fat. I suppose I must pay the ridiculous price of $1.40 for a sack of salt though, but mark my words . . . if ice cream is still marked $10 quart I shall walk right past the shop's cooler. We shall have to make do with potatoes and carrots." And pinning on her hat, she dashed out the back door.

Hugh's eyes were clouded with worry. He said, "Louisa, did you notice that my sister never glanced at Ashley. Each time she returns to our normal world she seems less and less aware of her own daughter."

The concern in his voice stabbed at my heart and I offered to watch over his niece while he was at the hospital. My offer pleased him, for he took my hand and kissed it which caused my heart to beat wildly like the beating wings of a hummingbird—how oddly my heart behaved, for hadn't it been numbed by the War?

*****

That night, around eight o'clock, I was sitting at the piano with Ashley when Hugh arrived home. Bloodstains darkened his shoes and I tried not to think of the horrors of a war-time hospital.

Charleen was in the kitchen baking a vegetable pie, so he closed the parlor door and sitting beside me he said, "I heard more news from the Peninsula. The Federals met no resistance from the Confederates until they reached Yorktown. McClellan has been stopped there by Confederate entrenchments that stretch across the entire width of the Peninsula."

I asked, "Was there a battle?"

He shook his head no and said, "For some unknown reason General McClellan has chosen to encamp his army in front of the Confederate's entrenchments instead of mounting an attack. Supposedly, thousands of Federals are now building their own entrenchments and emplacements for Union guns. I can't understand why McClellan prefers to put Yorktown under siege instead of advancing and fighting. His army is 100,000 men strong—he only faces Major General John B. Magruder's army of some 15,000 Confederates."

I reminded him: "Last night I told you that McClellan has a reputation for avoiding battles. Perhaps he fears fighting because he fears losing and spoiling his image as the Young Napoleon."

Hugh frowned and in a voice, deep with derision, he said, "Then McClellan is a fool. While he hesitates, the Confederacy acts boldly. Jeff Davis has a brilliant military advisor, a general named Robert E. Lee. There was talk at the hospital today that Lee has ordered General Joe Johnston to move his troops south to reinforce Magruder's army at Yorktown—"

Loud knocking interrupted him, and Hugh answered the front door. A Confederate officer stood on the step. A major. Major Robert Petrie. Hugh picked up Ashley and excusing himself, he went down the hall to the kitchen.

Major Petrie stood before me with the confidence of a man who had survived battles. He was a tall, handsome man with white-blond hair and a curly mustache; a very handsome man, indeed, but there wasn't a speck of conceit in his azure eyes or in his dazzling smile. He took my hand and bowed his head; his eyes resting for a moment on the brooch on my collar.

In a rich Georgian accent he asked, "Miss Holmes, I presume?"

I curtsied to him. "Major Petrie. I have been expecting you for days."

"I have been . . . occupied," he apologized most contritely. "If I had known I would be interviewing such a beautiful lady, I would have arrived sooner."

A smile came unbidden to my lips as I said, "I noticed, sir, that you have looked upon my brooch, so you know that I carry something that belongs to you." I took the watch from my pocket and giving it to him I added, "I am happy to place the watch in your care, Major Petrie. I worried that it was damaged during the crossing over the Potomac River, because I was drenched with water. Mr. Jones didn't realize, of course, or he would have been more careful as he rowed, but I worried that the watch would rust."

Deep lines creased his forehead. "I am distressed to learn of your discomfort during your crossing, Miss Holmes." He slipped the watch into the red sash of his uniform and smiled charmingly. "We will meet again in a few days, dear lady," and touching the brim of his hat he strode through the front door and disappeared into the night. Our interview took less than two minutes, but I was glad he hadn't stayed to open the watch in my presence—hopefully when he saw the smeared writing he would recall my words and blame the ruined message on Mr. Jones's careless rowing.

Chapter Sixteen

That night I was awakened by loud screams. A woman's screams. Terrified, I ran into the hallway towards Charleen's bedroom. Hugh had heard her screams too, for he flew up the stairs, and tried to open her door. It was locked. Hugh pounded with his fists, but his sister refused to turn the key.

The screams ended and after an eerie silence we heard laughter, weird, queer laughter, floating through the door. I looked at Hugh; perspiration wetted his forehead and his eyes widened with fear, for beyond the door we could hear Ashley whimpering with fright.

In a calmer voice Hugh called out, "Charleen . . . please open up . . ." and then the weird laughter faded into another silence before a key rattled and the door inched open. Charleen stood there as rigid as a tailor's mannequin; she wore her wedding gown, but it was tattered, shredded. In an unearthly voice she asked, "Has Peter sent for me? Tell him he must learn patience. My gown is torn and needs mending . . . tell Peter . . ." and then shuddering, she began to weep.

Gently, Hugh pulled the scissors from Charleen's hand and while he comforted her I edged around them towards the crib where Ashley was cowering against the bars. Tenderly, I gathered her up into my arms and carried her to my chamber where I sat with her in the rocking chair. After awhile she no longer trembled, but she kept her eyes on my face as though afraid I would disappear. Her eyes were so large with fright that my heart wept—this War has wrought fear in Ashley, an unnatural fear for a child—fear of her own mother.

CHAPTER SEVENTEEN

On the first Sunday of April I went to a late morning service at a church on Franklin Street. At the start of his homily, the pastor announced that three trains of soldiers under General Longstreet had arrived from Fredericksburg. He mentioned that the soldiers had not eaten for more than 24 hours and one by one people quietly left the pews. The pastor didn't complain as his church emptied because his parishioners were bent on charitable missions.

Instead of going home, I went to the shops on Broad Street—most had been closed for Sunday, but with the sudden arrival of the trains the shopkeepers opened their doors so that the citizens of Richmond could purchase food for the hungry soldiers. I, too, bought a basket and filled it with apples. I realized, of course, that my intention was to feed enemy soldiers— perhaps the very soldiers who had killed my Adam— but I couldn't stand by knowing that there were hungry men in need of help.

I carried my basket to a corner on Broad Street where others already waited for the hungry soldiers. Concerned women and children held loaves of white bread and plates of biscuits and muffins. One woman had filled her hat with tomatoes and another woman stood near a child's cart loaded with peppered hams. Flocks of girls, their cheeks blushed with excitement, giggled as they waited with pies and cakes.

When the soldiers appeared the giggling girls gazed with frank adoration, but when I looked upon the columns of grey uniformed soldiers my look was not of admiration. I thought . . . *here comes my enemy* . . . but as those soldiers came closer my heart ached for they looked as though they were ending a battle, not preparing for one. Their faces were blistered by the sun, and their uniforms were soiled and torn. They looked bone weary and wide eyed with hunger and I stepped off the curb and placed apples in their out-stretched hands.

The soldiers ate as though starved. Some of the soldiers ripped loaves of bread in half and tore off large bites. Other soldiers bit into whole cakes which smeared their faces with white frosting. One soldier pierced his bayonet through a roasted turkey and the soldiers behind him tore off pieces of meat like starving dogs tearing at a bone. Some soldiers were more thirsty than hungry and they held out their caps like cups for cold milk.

Up and down Broad Street bands played "Dixie" and in the neighboring houses ladies waved lacy handkerchiefs while small children saluted the soldiers. The music and cheering and marching soldiers reminded me of the parades of Washington—except for one important difference—those soldiers of the Confederacy were being applauded as they marched off to kill the soldiers of my beloved Union. After awhile I couldn't bear to watch anymore and I gave my basket to a soldier before I turned and slowly walked home.

That night I sat by my bedroom window and looked down at the hundreds of soldiers marching past. Supposedly some were marching towards Rocketts wharf where steamboats would carry them down river, while others were marching off to Shockoe Valley and other places where they would fight the Federals. I slept poorly that night, for I dreamed that the soldiers I fed that day killed the soldiers I had once fed in Washington. And yet, even when I awoke from that frightening dream, I knew it was my Christian duty to have fed those hungry men.

Over the next several days thousands of soldiers arrived in Richmond for their march down the Peninsula. They marched gayly with smiling faces and flower-strewn hats and high, eager steps. Throughout those days, as I watched the Confederates march out of Richmond toward distant battlefields, I decided that many of them had never tasted a major battle—otherwise their steps would have been less gay, less eager—for I remembered last summer when the soldiers of the Union had marched with equal enthusiasm towards Manassas and their slow return with frightened, bloodied faces. And so, as I watched the soldiers of the Confederacy, my heart was disquieted, for I dreaded the battle that would surely come.

CHAPTER EIGHTEEN

Early one evening, I accompanied Charleen to the shops to search for tea which had become scarcer as Mr. Lincoln's blockade of the South's ports tightened. As usual I pushed Ashley's pram, for Charleen had grown increasingly distanced from her little girl. Sadly, Ashley kept her eyes on her mother's face as though silently begging for attention.

We stopped outside the window of a butcher shop where wild turkeys hanged from their necks. Under the plump birds a sign read: Virginia's mountain turkeys—$4. Frowning, Charleen muttered, ". . . that price is outlandish." My offer to purchase a turkey insulted her and in a shrill voice she reminded me that I was her house guest, not boarder.

We entered the next door and greeted the shopkeeper; a kindly man with snow-white hair. When he turned to serve us we both gasped as Charleen cried out, "Mr. Clarkston, what happened to you?"

He spoke with obvious difficulty, for his lips were swollen grotesquely; both eyes were blackened and his neck was ringed with purplish bruises. In a hoarse voice he explained, "Last night as I was locking my door, a gang of thugs robbed me. I only carried a handful of coins, but I swear they would have beaten me with the same pleasure if my pockets had been empty."

I had heard about the gangs that roamed the streets of Richmond at night. Indeed, crimes against innocent citizens had become so common that the Confederate government started imposing restrictions on gambling houses and saloons to try and rid the city of rowdies. No street was safe after darkness fell. Often I worried about Hugh, for he left the hospital at late hours and I knew that he carried no weapon.

It was nearing dark, so the shopkeeper quickly filled Charleen's canister with black tea and we dashed home before the gangs started prowling the streets of Richmond.

When we arrived at the house Charleen went into the kitchen to prepare supper while I took Ashley upstairs to change her napkins. As I redressed her I thought about Charleen's constant struggle to feed all of us. Since my arrival in Richmond, she and her brother had refused my offers of money. Both were proud people, but I knew that the War had reduced their circumstances—Charleen was, of course, a widow with a small pension and Hugh was rarely paid for his services because most of his patients had been impoverished by the War (Charleen confided that her brother was sometimes paid with hay for his horse or with food, but usually he was given paper notes that promised future payments).

Of a sudden, I knew how I could help Charleen. I unclipped the money purse from my belt and placed ten dollars inside her sewing basket. She'd probably assume her brother had put the money there—if so, I could slip money into her basket whenever food was needed.

In a corner of the basket lay an ornate gold locket shaped like a heart; it hung on a long chain of gleaming gold. I opened the locket. On one-half of the heart was a miniature portrait of Charleen smiling beneath a veil of white lace; the other half showed a handsome man: her husband, Peter, no doubt. He, too, wore a smile. Their smiles saddened me, for on their wedding day they would never have known that war would separate them forever. I glanced over at the angelic face of their daughter and mourned them for their lost happiness. War is so unkind.

CHAPTER NINETEEN

A few nights later, Hugh arrived home late, but Charleen and I awaited supper for him. It was a dreadful meal as usual, of boiled potatoes and chick peas in a floury gravy. Hugh ate nothing; pushing his plate aside he said, "On my way home from the hospital I drove through mobs of men who are fired up with anger . . . Robert E. Lee has persuaded Jefferson Davis to sign into law, the Bill of Conscription. All white males between the ages of 18 and 35 years will now be drafted and each man must sign up for three years of military service."

"Why should that news anger the men of Richmond?" Charleen cried out. "Surely, the men of our glorious South are anxious to fight—"

"No, Charleen," Hugh interrupted, "there are many who have no desire to fight for the Confederacy . . . some simply fear battle, but some do not believe in this War."

Slowly Charleen rose from her chair; her knuckles whitened as she clenched her hands into fists. "You speak, brother, like a traitor."

Hugh looked wearily at his sister. "No, Charleen, I speak like an American who never wanted my country to divide into two separate nations. I speak as an American sickened by this bloody War."

Anger made Charleen's face hideous. Her eyes narrowed and flashed with vehemence and her mouth tightened into a flat line. In a louder, even shriller voice she asked, "Are you telling me, brother, that you refuse to enlist in the army of our illustrious Confederacy?"

"I am," he replied without hesitation.

"Then know this, my brother, that I am ashamed of you." She pushed back her chair so hard that it toppled over with a bang.

We listened as she stomped heavily up the steps and moments later a door slammed shut. Slipping off her own chair Ashley climbed up on Hugh's lap and pressed her face against his shoulder.

*****

For several days the streets of Richmond exploded with the noise of debate as people argued about the Bill of Conscription. Many, like Charleen, welcomed the draft as a patriotic duty, but equal numbers of people protested the bill as a violation—a violation against a man's right to choose for himself if he wished to serve in the military.

After five long days of outcry and protests, another act was published which listed ways in which a man could be excused from military duty. One excuse was given to men who owned a certain number of slaves. Yet, didn't the South declare this War on behalf of those slave owners? How strange that they should be excused.

Another way a man could be excused from military service was if he suffered from a disease or illness. Because of that, Hugh could not walk anywhere without men begging him to sign papers stating that they were crippled with rheumatism or suffered deafness or weak hearts.

Earlier today, I walked past the long lines of men waiting outside the draft board in the city's gasworks plant. Some stood with their heads held high as they waited to enlist as soldiers or sailors of the Confederacy. Others stood with lowered chins and stooped shoulders as they waited on crutches or with cotton-wrapped ears or with bandaged hands in their masquerade as sufferers of rheumatism, deafness or arthritis.

CHAPTER TWENTY

One morning a thin, white kitten wandered into our kitchen. Ashley squealed with delight and while the kitten lapped up a bowl of milk, she stroked him with a gentleness unusual in children her age—surely she has inherited her uncle's kind heart. For several days the kitten lingered around the house, drinking bowls of milk and following Ashley about, and as the kitten gained strength the rooms echoed with the soft sounds of Ashley's laughter and the kitten's purring. Then one afternoon the kitten wandered away. Ashley and I looked for the kitten throughout the neighborhood, but when darkness fell I took her home and sat by her crib until she cried herself asleep.

Charleen no longer welcomed my help in the kitchen, so when I went downstairs I was as surprised as Hugh when we found the dining room table festively set with china, goblets and candles. Hugh pulled out my chair and as I sat down I noticed that the table had been set for four.

Drawing by Joy Renee Maine

At that very moment, Charleen walked through the door, a steaming platter in her hands. She looked lovely; her gown was of blue satin and her hair was a wreath of curls tied up with ribbons. Around her neck hung the golden heart-shaped locket. Pulling out Charleen's chair, Hugh complimented his sister on her appearance.

Charleen murmured, "I must look my best, brother dear, for Peter has joined us for supper." And then she smiled at the empty chair that sat opposite her.

Hugh and I glanced at each other; it had been weeks since Charleen had drifted into that other world where her husband, Peter, was still alive.

Her eyes on the empty chair, Charleen said, "In honor of your homecoming, dear husband, I have prepared your favorite meal . . . veal loaf." Smiling sweetly, she placed a large slice of veal on the plate set in front of the empty chair. Her smile lingered as she gazed at the chair, at the husband who, she believed, sat there.

It was the first time that Charleen had served meat since my arrival, but my appetite disappeared as thousands of butterflies flittered about my stomach. Though sickened, I had no desire to offend her, and so I accepted the platter of veal and took a small portion.

Determined not to look at the empty chair, I stared down at my plate—the meat was covered with bits of white fur—the same white fur of the little kitten. Nauseous, I turned to Hugh and stumbling over my words I said, "My fa . . . my father kept cider in the cellar . . . would you . . . would you help me bring up a bottle?"

Her eyes on the empty chair, Charleen nodded as though in agreement to something that she heard before saying, "Peter and I would both enjoy a spirited drink with our supper . . . please, brother dear, help Louisa . . . that cellar is as dark as the grave."

Hugh followed me down the cellar steps without speaking. Clearly, his sister's illness troubled him, but when I lifted the lid of the garbage bin and pushed through the rubbish he asked, "Whatever are you looking for?"

I couldn't tell him. The words were too horrible to speak. Instead, I dug through the trash until I found a bundle of wet newspaper tied with string. The bundle stank terribly and another wave of nausea washed over me as I handed it to Hugh. Surely my behavior baffled him, but he broke the strings.

Under the folds of paper were the remains of the skinned kitten; its severed head and clumps of bloodied, white fur. Pressing my hands against my mouth I stepped back as Hugh dropped the awful bundle into the bin.

In a strangled voice he pleaded, "Please, Louisa, forgive my sister. She is more ill than I thought." And taking my arm he helped me up the cellar steps.

As I slipped past the dining room I heard Hugh explain my absence by saying that I was suffering a sudden headache and had retired for the evening. And then he added, "Charleen, I ate supper at the hospital . . . would Peter care for my portion of veal loaf?"

CHAPTER TWENTY-ONE

As the month of April closed, the newspapers reported that the Confederate city of New Orleans had fallen to the Union—New Orleans was the South's most important commercial port. Filled with new hope that the War would end soon, I flew on winged feet through the streets of Richmond. Everywhere I walked I heard men and women speak of New Orleans in anxious voices, but they seemed less concerned about a far-away city on the Mississippi River than about General McClellan's continued siege against Yorktown, only 60 miles down the Peninsula.

Throughout those weeks of siege Sammy, the shopkeeper's son, often delivered packages of food sent by ladies to beaus in the Confederate army, so I considered him a good source for news. That evening I hired him to carry my parcels home and along the way he shook the orange hair from his eyes and said, "You should see the Federals' balloons, Miss Holmes. Theys are bigger than a horse and they carries big baskets that soldiers ride in to the top of the sky."

I lifted my skirts to clear a puddle on the street before asking, "What do you think the balloons are for, Sammy?"

"For spying, Miss Holmes. Union soldiers spy down on our army. I brung a box of French candy from Miss Sally to her colonel friend and he let me fire his rifle at one of them balloons, but a cloud swallered it up."

When we reached the house I gave the chatty child another coin and cautioning him to take care on the darkening streets I opened the front door. Major Petrie was sitting in the parlor waiting for me.

CHAPTER TWENTY-TWO

Major Petrie rose to his feet and bowed when I entered the parlor. Strangely I felt quite calm as I closed the door and sat down.

Perhaps I felt composed because Major Petrie was a gentleman. Indeed, there was about him a romantic quality; a spirit of chivalry that ladies swoon over. Truly I rebuked myself for such thoughts—after all Major Petrie was my enemy—and yet, he was difficult to dislike for the light in his eyes revealed his joy for the uniform he wore—his clear eyes spoke of his devotion to the Confederacy. Thus, although he was misguided politically, he was, in my opinion, an honorable gentleman and therefore worthy of respect.

Major Petrie remained standing. He smiled at me (a most attractive smile) and pulled the pocket watch from the red sash of his officer's uniform. "Miss Holmes, it is my unfortunate duty to inform you that you must leave Richmond tonight. I have arranged passage on the boat, the *River Swan*, which is scheduled for departure at midnight. In two hours I will return with a carriage to escort you to the captain of the vessel. He, in turn, will deliver you into the hands of Mr. Jones who will row you back across the Potomac where Dr. Gleason is waiting." Major Petrie smiled again as he added, "Take care to keep the watch dry this time."

I took the pocket watch from him and asked, "Sir, why do you consider it your unfortunate duty to send me on my way?"

He kissed my hand and bowed again. "Because Richmond will be dull without your beauty." And without another word he was gone.

I parted the drapes and watched Major Petrie stride down the dark street. I couldn't help smiling, for he reminded me of one of those dashing heroes in an English novel of romance. Then my smile deepened as I recalled his words to keep the watch dry—his words told me that he had believed my fiction that the first message had been ruined during the crossing of the river—thus he must have hidden another message inside the watch. Hurrying upstairs I knocked at Hugh's door.

Luck was on my side; he was home from the hospital. I whispered, "Major Petrie just left. I must leave Richmond tonight."

My words brought a sudden change to Hugh's face, as though my words had cast a shadow over his heart. I wondered about that as he picked up his medical bag, took my arm and led me downstairs.

In the parlor he closed and locked the door while I sat at the desk and opened the back of the watch. Carefully, I removed the message as Hugh took the bronze disc from his medical bag and within minutes we had deciphered the letters,

HKTUV OGUUCIG PQV ENGCT. SWGUVKQP: YKNN
NKPEQNP TGRNCEG OEENGNNCP CU EQOOCPFGT
QH JKU CTOA?

to read:

FIRST MESSAGE NOT CLEAR. QUESTION: WILL
LINCOLN REPLACE MCCLELLAN AS COMMANDER
OF HIS ARMY?

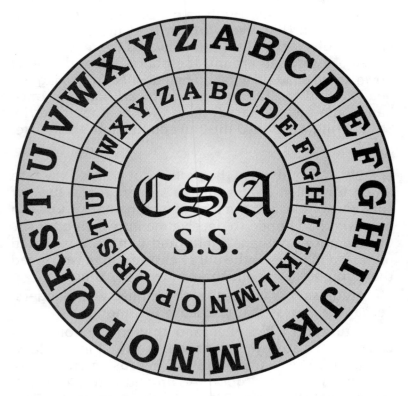

As I replaced the strip of paper inside the watch's chamber I said, "I won't do as Major Petrie wanted. I'll return to Washington by a different route—"

Loud pounding on the front door startled me and I slipped the bronze disc and watch into my pocket.

A policeman waited on the front step. "Dr. Ryle," he said, "you're needed immediately. A gang of men . . . Unionist rascals . . . have clubbed another man to a bloody pulp." He pointed at his horse where a man was slumped over the saddle.

Hugh darted down the steps even as he shouted, "Louisa, bring my bag." Quickly, I snatched up his medical bag and rushed outside where the policeman and Hugh were placing the injured man on the ground. Looking over at me, Hugh said, "Louisa, I won't need that after all. He's dead." Hugh kept his eyes on me and very discreetly he nodded towards the man's body. Puzzled, I stepped around the policeman and looked down at the dead man; blood had gushed from a jagged head wound to stain the man's blond hair and once handsome face. I stared. It was Major Robert Petrie. Shuddering, I dropped the bag and fled into the house.

*****

Hugh found me in the parlor, but I turned my face away, for I didn't want him to see my tears. I'm not sure why I mourned the loss of a man I hardly knew, a man who had hoped to deceive me into spying for the Confederacy—perhaps I mourned him because I had glimpsed in his eyes the pure heart of a man who loved the Confederacy as much as I loved the Union.

Hugh said, "Louisa, this city is filled with dangers. Perhaps it is best that you leave Richmond . . ."

I turned to him then and though my voice was choked with sorrow I managed to say, "I'm not leaving, Hugh. This War sickens me, because it violates all who are decent and good. Adam and Peter. Your sister and Ashley. Major Petrie. All the men of the Confederacy and Union. All the families of those good men who must bear their sorrow and loneliness with emptied hearts. No, Hugh, I shan't leave until I discover something of importance that can help Mr. Lincoln end this terrible War."

CHAPTER TWENTY-THREE

Early the next morning I began the first day of many days spying for the Union.

*****

On Sunday morning, the twenty-seventh of April, I prayed with the congregation at church for the citizens of New Orleans. Secretly I welcomed the Union's victory there, but my heart pitied the Southerners of that city on the Mississippi when I heard that General Benjamin Butler would act as their military governor. General Butler is known in Washington as the Beast, for his manner is vicious and cruel. The people of New Orleans will suffer under General Butler.

After the service Hugh drove me around the earthworks that edge the perimeter of Richmond. The earthworks—small mountains of red earth atop the hills and along the roads—are Richmond's final defense against Union attack.

Hugh rested his horse in the shadow of one mountain of earth; he told me that for several months he and other civilians had shoveled dirt until the mountain rose up before them. As Hugh turned the horse's head, we saw in the near distance a crowd of soldiers and citizens, both men and women, gathering near a gnarled tree; shovels and picks were slung over their shoulders.

*****

On Monday, a naval officer, an engineer named Captain Eugene Salkert, invited me to dine with him. Captain Salkert is connected with the Tredegar Iron Works—the foundry where the Confederacy manufactures cannons and weapons of all kinds. Although I thought him haughty, I accepted his invitation, in the hope he might disclose something of importance.

While we lunched I encouraged Captain Salkert to speak of his work at the foundry. He was a vain fellow and thus his boasting soon revealed a secret project—that very day the Confederates planned to test an underwater vessel called a submarine. I pretended disbelief, and as I hoped, he invited me to watch the test.

We drove to a spot on the river below Richmond where he pointed to an old fishing boat. Even as I watched, the boat exploded into a million pieces. Frightened, I looked around for cannons, but there were none to be seen.

Captain Salkert seemed amused by my fear as he declared that a submarine had caused the explosion. He explained that a torpedo mounted on a spar of the submarine had struck the underbelly of the fishing boat, thus causing the explosion.

I looked at the river, but I saw no ship, no vessel of any sort, and my wonderment about submarines grew as Captain Salkert ordered his driver to take us to Tredegar Iron Works. Once there, he took my arm and walked me through the yard towards a monstrous, bulbous, ugly-looking vessel—a submarine. Captain Salkert took delight as he revealed the submarine's sinister purpose: to blow up every ship in Mr. Lincoln's navy.

Later, upon my return home, I sketched the submarine in my journal and added all I had learned about that strange vessel that swims under water like a fish.

*****

The very next day, Tuesday, the twenty-ninth of April, was a day I shall never forget.

Hugh rose early and spent a long hour pacing the kitchen floor, for he was sorely troubled by a rumor that a prisoner from Castle Godwin had been moved to Camp Lee for execution. Hugh worried that one of his friends, Mr. Franklin Stearns or Reverend Alden Bosserman, might be that prisoner. I suggested that he drive to Camp Lee to learn the truth behind the rumor and he grabbed his hat and hurried from the house. While Hugh hitched his horse to the carriage I pleaded with him to take me along, for I knew he'd need moral support if the rumor proved true.

We arrived mid-morning at Camp Lee where a crowd of several hundred civilians, government officials and soldiers had gathered outside the walls. An inquisitive boy climbed like a monkey to the top of a high tree and he called down everything that he saw.

The boy shouted that a prisoner dressed in a black suit and silk dress hat was walking across the yard. Hugh's hand tightened on my arm as he strained to hear the boy's description of the prisoner; he still had no idea if the condemned man was one of his friends.

The boy called down that the prisoner walked calmly, bravely, up the steps and when he stood on the platform of the gallows he kept his chin high as the jailer bound his ankles and wrists together.

The boy shouted, "A minister is reading from the Holy Bible . . . a black hood has been put over the prisoner's head . . . the trap-floor has opened . . . the rope has failed . . . the prisoner has dropped to the ground . . . the guards have picked him up . . . he is being led up the steps again . . . another rope has been put around his neck . . . the trap has opened . . . he hangs by his neck."

And then, after a short silence, the boy yelled, "Someone has written the name of the dead man on the wall . . . Webster, Timothy Webster . . . Unionist spy."

Behind me a woman shouted, "Three cheers for the hangman! Hang all the Unionist spies!"

I closed my eyes as the cheers swelled around me; in my mind's eye I saw myself being led up the steps, and felt the coarse rope tightening around my neck and the floor giving way as the world darkened . . . I swooned and Hugh caught me in his arms and carried me through the cheering crowd.

I spoke nary a word as we drove back to Richmond, for fear silenced me—the fear that I, too, will be hanged as a spy.

✻✻✻✻✻

I slept poorly that night, for I dreamt that I was discovered as a spy and was hanged in front of a cheering crowd. When I awoke I stayed in my bedroom most of Wednesday, because I felt quite nauseous and my head whirled with pain. In truth, I suspected my illness was caused by my fearsome dream.

Thursday morning dawned with a brightness that gave me new courage. Perhaps my worst fears were dispelled because it was the first day of May, my favorite month of the year. I can't say why I felt braver that morning, but I cheerfully hired a carriage to carry me about as I spied.

Near the docks I happened upon a long line of black carriages that were closely followed by wagons overfilled with trunks and baggage. Curious, I bid my driver to park near the quay where I watched as men in fine suits and ladies in crinoline gowns stepped down from the carriages and dashed up the gangplanks of flat-bottomed boats.

My driver, a gabby fellow, recognized the gentlemen as members of the Congress of the Confederate States. Apparently he respected none of them, for he spat on the pavement and muttered, "Look at those rascals scurrying up those gangplanks like water rats . . . they voted to give themselves generous pay raises, and now they're deserting Richmond with their belongings and their women."

In a short time all the vessels were fully loaded and long ropes were tied to fat mules; a whistle sounded and the mules plodded up the canal, towing the boats behind them. My driver may have been angered at the sight of his congressmen fleeing the city, but their flight pleased me—surely the Confederate government fled because they expected the Federals to invade and capture Richmond.

*****

Friday was a fairly quiet day, but on Saturday, May 3, the city erupted with the noise of frightened voices— the citizens of Richmond were alarmed by the news that General Joe Johnston had quietly abandoned Yorktown in the early morning hours. Reportedly there had been no struggle, no battle, no bloodshed. The general simply pulled his army out of Yorktown and began a slow march through the mud towards Richmond. In the wake of Johnston's army, General McClellan's army of Federals took possession of Yorktown.

As I made my way about the streets I heard the same question asked over and over by the citizens of

Richmond: Why did General Johnston suddenly withdraw from Yorktown after keeping the Federals from advancing up the Peninsula for a month? Many criticized their general and for good reason—Johnston's abandonment of Yorktown had forced the Confederates to desert their naval base in Norfolk before the Federals could arrive there and confiscate Confederate ships for the Union's navy.

As I walked home my feet felt as light as feathers, for happiness made me feel like dancing. McClellan's possession of Yorktown had pushed the Federals a step closer to Richmond. A step closer to the end of this dreadful War.

*****

On Sunday, May 4, I accompanied Charleen and Hugh to their church for the noon service. Charleen walked far ahead of Hugh and me; we followed more leisurely since we held Ashley's hands and she insisted on walking by herself.

As we slowly walked along I kept my eyes on those around me, for it had become my custom to carefully observe everyone I saw. What I noticed that morning was that *fear* marked the faces of all those we passed. You could feel their *fear* as though it were a living, breathing thing that had invaded the streets of Richmond. Such *fear* could only have one cause: the steady approach of General McClellan's army.

We reached St. Paul's Church in time for the service, but it was so crowded that we went upstairs to the balcony. Ashley sat on her uncle's knee and leaning over the railing, she waved her tiny hand at the ladies and gentlemen seated below.

During the service, the minister, a Reverend Minnigerode, invited the candidates for Confirmation to approach the chancel. A tall gentleman rose from his seat and strode towards the minister and when he turned to face the congregation I stared in utter amazement. That gentleman was none other than President Jefferson Davis. He was followed to the altar by several Confederate officers and then everyone bowed their heads as the men received the Holy Sacrament of Confirmation.

*****

The following day, Monday, the fifth of May, we heard news of a battle that was taking place on the Peninsula. The street gossips reported that General McClellan's advance troops were fighting against General Johnston's rear guard troops that were entrenched at Williamsburg.

We learned no further news of Williamsburg until Friday, May 9, when the battle was written up in the newspaper—McClellan's Federals had taken over Williamsburg.

Hugh arrived home by supper time with more news. He had heard that the Confederacy did not view the battle at Williamsburg as a defeat. Indeed, the Confederacy didn't even consider the battle a battle! Instead, Williamsburg was described as a mere delaying tactic that supposedly taught McClellan a harsh lesson—not to interfere with the retreat of a Confederate army.

How could the Confederacy deny that a battle had taken place? The newspaper reported that the Federals suffered terrible casualties of 2,200 men and the South suffered 1,700 casualties! I will never understand the definitions of war.

For the past several weeks Charleen had been acting quite normal. In all those weeks she never once slipped into that other world, the World of Insanity. That particular Friday evening, she seemed in especially fine spirits as she sat in the parlor singing to her daughter. Hugh was delighted with his sister's health of mind, and so he accepted an invitation to a supper party. He asked me to accompany him and I readily agreed even though he refused to tell me where we would dine.

I wore the most elegant gown I had brought; a French gown of lemon silk that was the same color as my hair. When Hugh saw me he said not a word, but instead, stepped outside into the back garden. He returned a moment later with a spray of lemon blossoms and Charleen helped me pin the flowers into my hair. Taking Hugh's arm we walked down the path towards his carriage.

As we drove through the lamplit streets I stole a glance at him; under the moon's light the yellow in his hair flickered like bits of golden fire. He caught my eye and smiled, and suddenly the night took on a magic of its own as the stars abandoned the heavens and illuminated his blue eyes. I thought him splendid, wonderful. In the past weeks I had learned of his reputation as a skilled surgeon, I had witnessed his gentleness with his sister, with Ashley and with the ill who called at the house, and I had observed him in moments of sadness when he spoke of this War and in other moments of laughter when he forgot this War. He seemed to have lived a lifetime already and yet, he was only nineteen years of age. Perhaps War ages the young beyond their years, for he possessed unusual maturity even though his face bore the freshness of youth in the vivid colors of his eyes and hair and in the confidence of his smile.

We turned onto Church Street and pulled up before the gates of President Jefferson Davis's mansion. Hugh understood my pleasure, because he knew what I realized at once—that I might overhear an important remark that could be recorded in my journal.

We were greeted by President Davis and his wife, Varina. By all measures, she was a lovely woman; her round face and soft smile lent serenity to her features, while her eyes revealed keen intelligence. Often she glanced lovingly at her husband and apparently he was equally devoted to her, for he stayed at her side throughout the evening—I should know since I kept my spying eyes on both of them.

President Davis appeared distracted; whenever someone spoke to him he didn't respond at first as though his mind dwelt on other things. As I watched, a messenger came into the drawing room and asked President Davis for a private moment. After they had spoken the president drew his wife aside and whispered something that caused her face to whiten.

I looked around for Hugh, hoping he knew the messenger's news, but a portly gentleman stepped in front of me, barring my way. Forcing his company on me he droned on about his tobacco plantation in North Carolina; indeed, his breath smelled of foul cigars. Coughing, I beseeched him for a glass of punch and when his back was turned I escaped into the garden.

I sat on a bench in the shadow of a lilac bush and breathed in the night's perfumed air. In the quiet I heard a man and woman speaking in lowered voices. Even as I rose to announce my presence, I realized how foolish that would be since I might overhear something of importance. So, I sat very still and eavesdropped without shame.

I soon recognized the voices as those of President Davis and his wife, Varina. In a clear and frightened tone she whispered, "Dearest husband, I dread leaving you . . . we might never see each other again . . . no, I cannot . . . I will not leave you."

I heard the sound of a kiss before Mr. Davis said, "Sweet wife, you must take the children and leave tomorrow . . . you will be safe in Raleigh. If our navy can block the Union's fleet from reaching Richmond you may return here. I promise you that, but tonight after our guests leave, you must finish your packing."

Varina made some sort of reply, but I couldn't understand her words and then I realized that she was weeping. I had heard enough. Although this was War,

I felt horrid listening to a private conversation between husband and wife, and so I slipped back inside the house and asked Hugh to drive me home at once.

When we closed the front door we heard a crash in the kitchen. Hugh darted down the hall, and I followed with dread in my heart.

Charleen stood in the middle of the room with a plate in her hand. All around her the floor was littered with broken crockery and shattered glassware. She threw the plate against the wall even as she jerked her face towards us; her eyes had narrowed into slits and spittle wet her chin when she spat, "Have you heard the news? Our navy has deserted Norfolk. Today that ugly baboon Abraham Lincoln walked about Hampton Roads congratulating his generals and troops." She grabbed a cup and smashing it against the stove she screamed, "I despise Lincoln and all Northerners . . . before the Yankees come to Richmond I will destroy this very house . . . they'll never have this roof over their heads."

Hugh grasped his sister by the wrists and spoke to her in a soothing voice until she calmed down enough to be led upstairs. I stood quietly, numbed by the sight of the broken china—my grandmother's china—that was part of my childhood. A few minutes later Hugh returned and placing a comforting arm around my shoulders he apologized for his sister's destructive tantrum. He promised, most kindly, to replace the pieces, but childhood memories cannot be replaced.

We swept the floor together. Afterwards, as I looked at the shattered pieces of a china figurine of a maiden, I considered gluing it back together, but there were too many pieces to mend. A sudden thought came to me that Charleen was like the china maiden, for her mind had been shattered by the War—perhaps too shattered to ever mend.

*****

In the early hours of Saturday, May 10, Mrs. Davis and her children piled their luggage on a train and left for Raleigh. When Charleen heard, she flew into another rage and branded Mrs. Davis a cowardly wife. I knew better of course, for I had heard the agony in Varina's voice when she had begged her husband to let her remain at his side.

The citizens of Richmond were alarmed by the departure of Mrs. Davis and her children because they took her hasty departure as a sign that Richmond was in mortal danger. Alarm rapidly turned into action as some citizens followed Mrs. Davis's example and fled Richmond. When the family next door, the Dufours, began to load their belongings on a wagon Charleen flew at them like an angry hen. She accused Mr. Dufour of being a traitor before slapping his wife's face and screaming bitter words at his small children.

For much of that afternoon Charleen railed and cursed about Mr. Lincoln and the Union. Eventually I carried Ashley upstairs to my chamber, so she could play with her doll in quiet while I wrote about the *fear* that plagued Richmond. Afterwards, I took great care to hide my journal—unquestionably, if Charleen found it she would turn her rage against me.

*****

On Sunday evening Hugh came home from the hospital with a copy of the newspaper, *Examiner*. He seemed rather excited as he showed me an article written by a reporter named Moses Hoge. The story read,

. . . today . . . the C.C.S. *Virginia* was scuttled . . .

I looked at Hugh and asked, "Why does that ship's name sound so familiar?"

He lowered his voice so that Charleen wouldn't hear. "You know that ship by the name, *Merrimack* . . . she fought against the Union's ironclad, *Monitor* . . . the battle in which your sister's beau was blinded."

Taking the newspaper from me he read Moses Hoge's words:

> . . . the Confederate government has found nothing better to do with the *Merrimack*—that great gift of God and of Virginia to the South—than to take her out into the river and blow her timbers to atoms . . .

Utterly confused, I asked, "Why did the Confederacy destroy such a valuable ship?"

Hugh explained, "When the Confederates abandoned their navy yard at Norfolk the *Merrimack* couldn't be moved to safety because the waters were too shallow. The ironclad had to be destroyed before the Federals reclaimed her for their own navy."

And then in his lowered voice Hugh read from Hoge's article:

> . . . the *Monitor*, two other Federal ironclads, the *Naugatuck* and the *Galena*, and an escort of Union gunboats are moving towards Richmond. Their purpose is clear: to shell Richmond until this city surrenders . . .

Hugh's eyes flashed with excitement when he whispered, "Louisa, when Richmond surrenders, this bloody War will finally end."

*****

At the close of each day, I closeted myself in my chamber and recorded all I had seen and heard in my journal. As the pages filled up I knew I would have to eventually leave Richmond, so as to deliver the journal to Mr. Lincoln. And yet, I couldn't bear the thought of leaving Richmond. Or Hugh.

CHAPTER TWENTY-FOUR

For days the people I passed on my daily walks looked almost dazed as though they wore *Masks of Fear*. Their *fear* was wrought by gruesome reports about the cruel treatment of the Confederate citizens of New Orleans by the Union's military governor, Major General Benjamin Butler—the man I knew as the Beast. Supposedly he had hanged a civilian for merely lowering a Union flag and he had issued an order to the ladies of that city—if they acted or spoke rudely to any Federal soldier they would be treated with the same disrespect paid to painted ladies.

As the stories of Butler's monstrous acts in New Orleans swept through Richmond, the citizens *feared* equal cruelty if their city fell into Union hands. Such *fears* caused the citizens to react in one of two ways: some chose to fight alongside the Confederate army while others chose flight from Richmond.

Those who chose to fight took up weapons of rakes or sticks or rifles and headed down river to stand beside Johnston's soldiers.

And those who chose flight nailed boards across windows and chained padlocks on doors before driving off in wagons piled with goods from homes and shops. For several days and nights the streets were mobbed with wagons headed south while the piers along the river were jammed with flat boats carrying families and their belongings to western ports.

Each day *fears* grew stronger as the *Monitor* and other Federal ships moved slowly up the James River blasting their powerful guns at towns and plantations. As the Union flotilla drew even closer to Richmond the citizens grew more panic-strickened and one by one shops and churches and houses were abandoned. Strangely, as the townspeople evacuated the city, refugees from the countryside streamed into Richmond, for they believed they would find safety in the capital city of their Confederacy.

*****

Each night, when the hour grew late, it became my custom to wait for Hugh to arrive home from the hospital. Then, while he ate supper, we discussed the War. We always took care to speak in lowered voices since we were ever mindful of Charleen who passed her evenings sewing in the parlor. Irregardless, those hours spent by the kitchen hearth were pleasant hours for both Hugh and me, truly pleasant hours.

One night, Hugh arrived home with such a weary look on his face that I thought him ill at first. I hung his rain-soaked coat by the hearth and made him sit in the rocker while I poured him a cup of honeyed tea. He watched me without saying a word and I knew he was sorely troubled. In a bare whisper he told me, "The Federal flotilla will soon reach Richmond. They have destroyed the Confederate battery at Rock Wharf and have already passed Hardin's Bluff and Jamestown . . . the flotilla can't be stopped . . . some Confederate sharpshooters hid on the edge of an old river plantation with the hope of ambushing the Union boats, but the Confederates were all killed by cannonballs fired from the Federal ironclad, *Galena*."

Wearily Hugh rubbed his hand across his eyes and said, "This morning I attended one of Robert E. Lee's officers . . . he had the swamp fever . . . the poor man was wracked with chills, but he needed to talk and so I listened . . . he said that some members of President Davis's Cabinet asked General Lee if Richmond should be abandoned before the arrival of the Federal flotilla. The officer told me that General Lee had tears in his eyes when he rebuked the Cabinet saying, 'Richmond must not be given up; it shall not be given up!'"

Mindful of Charleen's near presence I whispered, "Hugh, you seem troubled by the approach of the Federal flotilla. Why?"

Hugh put his cup on the table and for a long while he stared at the cold ashes on the hearth floor before saying, "Louisa, what kind of monster am I to delight in the news that the flotilla approaches this city and will probably shell it into ashes . . . what kind of monster am I?"

I put my hand on his. "You are not a monster, Hugh. You merely want this War to end . . . you know that once Richmond falls, the Confederacy will collapse and peace will come again. As for the people of this city, Hugh, take comfort in the fact that although General McClellan is a vain, egotistical man, he has none of the cruel manners of General Butler. McClellan won't destroy this city or harm her citizens if she surrenders."

Hugh shook his head sadly. "You don't understand the pride of these people, Louisa . . . even if McClellan doesn't destroy Richmond, the citizens will burn down this city before McClellan sets foot on a single street. Already there is talk of torching homes and the capitol building and even the statue of George Washington before McClellan's invasion. Mayor Mayo is registering boys younger than 18 years and men older than 45 years to join his Home Guard—they will take any weapon they can find and fight to the death. Believe me, the citizens of Richmond will refuse to surrender to McClellan—their stubborn pride will be this city's death warrant."

*****

The next morning, Thursday, May 15, I woke to the soft thunder of guns from the south. I dressed hurriedly and rushed outside where I saw Hugh leading his horse and carriage from the side yard into the street. Worry creased his eyes as he said, "Louisa, the Union flotilla is a mere seven miles from Richmond . . . near a place called Drewry's Bluff . . . I am going there in case a doctor is needed."

"Please take me with you," I begged him and perhaps because he heard the urgency in my voice he agreed and within minutes we were on our way out of Richmond.

*****

Drewry's Bluff is a hill nearly 100 feet above the James River. We left the carriage in a stand of trees and climbed the hill towards a detachment of Confederates who manned eight large cannons. The massive guns were pointed at the water below.

Down river, perhaps a mile away, a flotilla of ships steamed towards Drewry's Bluff.

Hugh's presence was never questioned (truly a doctor's medical bag is a passport) and I was mistaken for his nurse. We were told to stand on the far side of a bronze cannon where we spoke to an excited sailor. Pointing down at a pile of boulders he explained, "Hiding down there on either side of the river are companies of sharpshooters who are waiting for them Union ships . . . they aim to shoot every man off every deck." He spat and added, "And down there where the river narrows and turns sharp, we sank old ships, dropped tons of rock and drove in pilings—those obstacles will stop the Federal ships from reaching Richmond."

I shivered at the thought of the cannons that would soon fire down on my nation's ships . . . if only I could have warned the Federals, but how? How? I shook violently, dreading the slaughter that was about to happen whilst the sailor stared at me as though he knew somehow that I was a Unionist. Fear of discovery made me blurt out, "Tell me, sir, why you and your fellow sailors are fighting on land and not on water?"

He narrowed his eyes at me. "Miss, I had a ship once . . . the ironclad *Virginia* (he meant, of course, the *Merrimack*) . . . a few days ago, when we deserted the navy yard at Norfolk we couldn't move the *Virginia* through the shallow waters to safety . . . so four days ago, on May 11, I helped load that great ship with explosives and watched as she blew apart . . . after the *Virginia* exploded, me and the other men of my crew traveled by train to Richmond to help defend our capital. We intend to blast the Federal's flotilla out of the water."

He looked towards the flotilla of Federal ships as though hungry for battle and I, too, looked down as the ships of my nation steamed closer and closer towards the bend—the bend in the river where the cannons were pointed and where the sharpshooters were loading their rifles.

Moments later the first guns opened up and I ran down the hill towards the carriage. I sat there covering my ears with my hands, hating each clap of a cannon and each pop of a rifle and I wept as those horrible sounds of war surrounded me.

Hours passed before the guns grew silent and in their place I heard cheering from atop the hill. I knew what those cheers meant even before I saw Hugh walking slowly down the hill towards me. He put his bag in the back of the carriage and untying the reins from the tree he climbed onto the seat. He spoke not a word to me as he studied my face and then wiping the tears from my eyes he took me into his arms and said, "Richmond has been saved. The *Monitor* couldn't lift her guns high enough to reach the top of Drewry's Bluff and the *Naugatuck's* parrot gun apparently burst only minutes after the battle began. Only the ironclad *Galena* fought back . . . for three hours she was hit repeatedly before she was forced to move back downstream. The fleet of wooden boats moved with her . . . it was a terrible sight to see, Louisa . . . the Confederate's sharpshooters and heavy cannons did a great deal of damage."

The cheers from the hill swelled even louder and snapping the reins Hugh turned the carriage around towards Richmond.

CHAPTER TWENTY-FIVE

By the time our carriage reached Richmond, the news of the Confederate victory at Drewry's Bluff was known on every street. Amazingly, all the *fear* that had invaded the city during the past weeks drifted away like the smoke of a dying fire; men tore boards away from shop windows and threw open padlocked doors while, almost magically, ladies appeared in spring gowns and children played on lawns with dolls and balls. Even Charleen seemed lighter of heart, for she greeted us at the gate with a radiant smile as she called out, "Have you heard the news of Drewry's Bluff?"

Hugh nodded and jumping down from the carriage he came around to my side and helped me down.

Charleen darted through the gate and grabbing her brother's arm, she cried out, "I said, brother dear, have you heard the good news? The Federal flotilla has been turned back. We must celebrate with a grand supper . . ." Her joy vanished as she stared up at Hugh's face. "There's no pleasure in your face, brother." Spinning around towards me she stared at my face. "Nor yours, Louisa." Understanding came to her and her face bleached white as she hissed, "Traitors. Both of you are traitors." Her voice grew shrill as she screamed, "Traitors! Traitors!"

Taking his sister by the arm Hugh forced her into the house and as I shut and locked the front door I heard him say, "Charleen, do you want me to be arrested? Who would take care of you and Ashley?"

She stopped screaming then, but for the rest of the day she glared at us and refused to speak a single word. Later, after supper, she turned to her evening custom of sewing in the parlor. Usually she sewed sandbags for Confederate fortifications—first for Yorktown, then for Williamsburg and more recently for Richmond, but that night she put aside the sandbags to cut strips of cloth into bandages. Stubbornly she kept her silence, but as she worked she smiled; her smile was as cold as death.

*****

Celebrations of the victory at Drewry's Bluff erupted all over the city. Amid those celebrations the citizens seemed to forget that their half-starved, exhausted army was retreating back through the mud towards Richmond—and that the powerful army of the Union followed in their very footsteps. And the citizens seemed to forget that Union ships prowled the James River and the York River on either side of their Peninsula. The citizens forgot all that until the day General Johnston camped his army a mere five miles outside Richmond.

It was rumored that President Davis questioned his general's wisdom of camping the army on the outskirts of Richmond—he wanted Johnston to move his army down the Peninsula towards the Chickahominy

River. Johnston refused—perhaps he reasoned that the river would prevent a retreat if one became necessary. Whatever the general's reason, it was rumored that his soldiers welcomed his stubborn refusal to camp closer to the river (supposedly the troops dreaded the Chickahominy for it overflows with poisonous snakes and mosquitoes and swamp disease swirls over its smelly waters).

*****

As the days of May unfolded, our meals became more wretched. Much of the food in the market was sent to the starving soldiers, so we ate what could be found. I suspected that Charleen fed us rats and dead birds, but we ate hungrily.

When a newspaper reported that McClellan's Federal army feasted on rich foods Charleen flew into a rage—I sympathized with her though because Ashley had grown thin and frail. Her round face had narrowed which made her eyes seem even larger; indeed, her once bright eyes had dulled and were ringed by black circles. She rarely played with her rag-doll, and she no longer smiled. Every morning and night Hugh fed her spoonfuls of castor oil, and I knew by the worry in his eyes that he feared Ashley was dying.

*****

By May 20, the army of General McClellan had crossed the Chickahominy River. According to the street gossips, President Davis ordered General Johnston to engage McClellan in battle immediately while the Federals had the river at their back since the river would cut off the Union's avenue of escape. To make matters worse for the Federals, the heavy rains of May had swelled the river—even I, a civilian untrained in warfare, understood that if the Chickahominy flooded its banks, the Federals would have to face two deadly enemies—the Confederate army and the drowning waters of the river.

On the streets of Richmond there was anxious talk—most of the men and women spoke about the siege that they believed would soon come. Siege of Richmond meant one certainty—starvation until the city surrendered. I knew that Ashley would die if there were a siege, for she would never be able to survive on stews of boiled leather. As much as I wanted Richmond to fall, I couldn't bear the thought of that darling child starving to death.

*****

On the morning of Friday, May 30, I woke feeling as though I were suffocating. I pushed away the bed clothes and opened my window, but the air that met me was hot and moist.

With each passing hour the day grew increasingly hot as the clouds billowed and darkened and long, rolling thunder exploded in the heavens. Far away, the skies were split by yellow bolts of lightning as black clouds scudded through the greenish sky. The storm frightened Ashley and she crawled under the kitchen table and cried, but Charleen ignored her and sat by the window with an odd smile that seemed to welcome the storm. I picked up Ashley and she clung to me in terror; indeed I shared her fear, for the storm seemed unnatural, evil.

The winds came suddenly as branches snapped off trees and rubbish cans rolled down the streets. The shutters banged against the front windows and I knew I had to lock them before the glass shattered. Forcing Charleen to hold her daughter, I ran outside. As I closed and fastened the shutters over the windows the wind whipped at my skirts and pushed me to and fro, but somehow I kept my balance until each window was covered. It was then that ugly, jagged lightning arced out of the clouds and terrified, I ran inside the house.

I found Ashley whimpering near the front door; Charleen stood by the parlor hearth, still smiling that strange smile as she stared up at her husband's sword. I spoke to her, but she didn't answer me, and so I took Ashley into the kitchen and rocked her to sleep by the hearth.

The hours of that day passed slowly. While Ashley was awake I coaxed her to eat porridge and then I read to her or played with her until she fell asleep on a bed of pillows near the hearth. While she slept I sat near her under the kitchen window and watched the rains pour from the clouds. Throughout those long hours Charleen never left the parlor and I was relieved that she kept to herself.

After midnight Hugh returned from the hospital. He was drenched from the rains and while he sat by the hearth I prepared him some coffee and stewed rhubarb. He ate hungrily and when he had finished he said, "One of General Johnston's majors visited the wounded tonight. He announced his belief that the storm was sent from heaven to cause chaos in McClellan's camp—spies reported that lightning killed several Federal soldiers and that the rains have flooded the Chickahominy River."

Hugh stood up and staring through the window at the rain he said, "Louisa, I eavesdropped on the major when he spoke to a fellow officer . . . he told him that the floods have washed away most of the bridges that span the Chickahominy. In essence, the Federals camped on this side of the river have been cut off from the rest of McClellan's army. General Johnston plans to use this stroke of fate to his advantage . . . he plans to attack the isolated units of McClellan's army in the morning . . . he is gambling that those damaged bridges will prevent Union reinforcements from reaching those units—"

Hugh paused then as though unwilling to say what he had to say and walking over to the hearth he looked down at Ashley for a long moment. His face looked aggrieved and when he turned towards me he spoke in a voice almost too low to hear. He said, "Louisa, the hospital has asked me to volunteer as a field surgeon during the battle. I am comforted knowing you are here watching over my niece and sister. I—" But he left his sentence unfinished and putting on his hat he walked out the back door.

Ice covered my heart. Perhaps it was the expression on Hugh's face or the tone of his voice or perhaps it was his unfinished sentence that chilled my heart. For hours I sat by the window and watched as flashes of lightning lit up the sky while I tried to convince myself that the storm was not an omen of evil. Of death.

✶✶✶✶✶

Saturday morning dawned with grey skies and heavy clouds. Ashley woke soon after; I checked her napkins, but she was dry which worried me because her napkins were usually soaking wet. I mixed some pumpkin paste with warm milk and honey and she ate willingly which quieted my worries that she was ill. Unfortunately, when Charleen came into the kitchen Ashley dropped her spoon and hid her face.

I, too, felt like hiding because Charleen was carrying her husband's sword. She greeted neither her daughter nor me as she took a rag and wiped the blade of the sword. Uneasy, I watched her carefully, trying to decide if she was in that faraway world where her husband still lived when she muttered, "Last night Peter told me to polish his sword. He shall fight a battle today."

Her words horrified me. Picking up Ashley I put her in her pram and quietly wheeled her out the back door. Thunder sounded in the skies above, but we were safer in a storm than in the house with Charleen while she lived in that other world, of insanity.

Thunder boomed again and again and I turned off the street into a hotel to take shelter, but the thunder caused the walls to shake and the windows to rattle. Afraid that the building would collapse I rushed outside to the pavement, uncertain where to go. As I stood there a boy ran by shouting that the battle had begun—it wasn't thunder that had rattled the windows—it was the roar of cannons.

All at once the street was crowded with men and women and children running towards the hills outside Richmond—they hoped to glimpse the battle. I turned the pram into the crowd and joined the exodus towards the hills.

It was awkward pushing the pram over the thick grasses, but before long I stood amidst the others atop a small hill. To the east could be seen the thick smoke of cannons, but it was impossible to tell if the smoke spewed from Southern or Northern cannons. As I watched, I prayed continuously for Union victory; at times my prayers were interrupted by cheers when the crowd believed that Confederate cannons had fired, while at other times the crowd grew deathly quiet when it was believed that Union cannons had fired.

Ashley sat in her pram contentedly listening to the popping sounds that floated towards us, but the sounds didn't amuse me for I recognized them as the sounds of rifles and muskets. I thought constantly of Hugh for he carried a medical bag instead of a weapon—and yet I knew that surgeons are targeted as well as any man on a battlefield.

A gentleman dressed in civilian clothes galloped madly away from the battlefield; when he came closer, he slowed his horse and someone grabbed at his reins and demanded news. The rider, who happened to be a newspaper reporter from the *Examiner*, yelled, "The Confederates are charging into McClellan's divisions and are forcing them back at Seven Pines. The Confederates are winning!"

Sickened by the news I stood stiffly as the hours passed while Confederate soldiers straggled past; some of them were wounded and some were simply fatigued, but none of them were willing to tell further news from the fields of battle. After some time Ashley sobbed with hunger, but a kindly lady gave her a boiled potato and a tin of milk. Later as I rocked Ashley to sleep in her pram, I stared across the miles at the dust and smoke of battle and my prayers changed—I prayed for all those who fought—the brave men of the blue army and the equally brave men of the grey army.

At some point, I'm not sure when for time seemed to stop, some soldiers passed by carrying a stretcher bearing a wounded officer; the man's shoulder and chest were wrapped in white cotton that was smeared with blood. Upon seeing the officer's face, a lady gasped, "We are lost . . . General Joe Johnston has been wounded!"

Hope for a Union victory flooded over me and worried that my smile would reveal me as a Unionist, I pushed the pram down the hill towards Richmond.

*****

Late that afternoon Ashley felt feverish, so I placed her in the kitchen tub and splashed cool water over her warm back and face. Afterwards, I wrapped her in a blanket and placed a bag of freshly cut mint on her forehead, but she burned with the fever and cried miserably. Suddenly, the door burst open and Charleen strode into the kitchen with her arms crossed and her face rigid. "Shut your brat up, missy," she hissed, "or I will force you from my house. My husband is expected any minute and he deserves a quiet home."

Charleen was dressed beautifully, but in the past weeks she had lost so much weight that her gown hung on her like a shroud. I thought, *she thinks Ashley is my child*, and so I carried Ashley upstairs to my chamber and stayed with her until she fell asleep. Her forehead felt cooler after the bath, but I worried that the fever would return.

While Ashley slept I went downstairs to prepare fresh bags of crushed mint. I kept one eye on Charleen as she filled the iron with hot coal so as to finish pressing a white shirt—a shirt that once belonged to her husband. The silence in the kitchen was heavy. Perhaps that's why we heard the noise out on the street.

Slamming down the iron Charleen cried out, "Peter's home!" She darted down the hall and I followed with dread weighing my heart. I came upon her standing in the open door with her head lowered and her shoulders sagging—because, of course, Peter had not arrived home.

Instead, the street was jammed with wagons loaded with bloodied soldiers who groaned out loud in their misery and pain. Other carts passed by filled with soldiers, but those soldiers made no sound for they, poor souls, had been muted by death. Soldiers who were still able to walk or limp or even crawl into town followed the wagons. Civilians, walking alongside the wounded, lent shoulders to lean upon or hands to half-carry or half drag those whose strength had failed. The noise was deafening: the rumbling of wagons, the groaning of men, the shouting of officers, and the weeping of women. Above all the noise I heard singing, as soldiers and civilians sang "Dixie."

There seemed no end to the procession of wounded trudging up the street. A man mounted on a mule rode back and forth shouting that the hospitals were crowded and telling the soldiers to go to the warehouses along the river . . . or to find shelter where they could. Some of the wounded listened to him and simply moved off the road and dropped onto the sidewalks.

As I watched, memories of last summer flooded over me; memories of Union soldiers, defeated and broken, straggling into Washington after the Battle of Bull Run. I remembered that I had invited the wounded and the weary of the Federal army to come onto my lawn and porch—I could do no less for the wounded and weary of the Confederate army. Pushing past Charleen I flung open the front gate and invited the soldiers into my home.

Within the hour twenty wounded soldiers were settled in the bedrooms on the second floor, while others lay on blankets spread on the porch. Scores of other soldiers who suffered exhaustion collapsed onto the lawn to sleep. Indeed, all of the soldiers, the wounded and the unwounded, slept soundly which was merciful for I had neither food nor medicines to offer.

Oddly, the presence of all those soldiers brought Charleen back into our normal world. The motherly side of her nature came out and she fretted that many of the wounded would need her brother's care, so she generously suggested that we turn her chamber into a surgery. In turn, I invited her to move her belongings into my chamber and together we carried Ashley's crib and their clothes down the hall. As we worked together I thought how lovely and kind Charleen could be when her mind was healthy—how sad that the War had wounded her mind.

We had just finished hanging Charleen's dresses in my wardrobe when Ashley awoke, her cheeks the color of crimson. Charleen picked up her daughter (she again recognized Ashley as her own child), and while I filled the tub in the kitchen she gently removed Ashley's fever-wet clothes.

In spite of cooling baths, Ashley's fever remained high. As I chopped mint and filled small bags, I prayed that Hugh would return home, for surely he would have medicines that could rid Ashley of sickness.

Drawing by Joy Renee Maine

When night fell Charleen told me that our cupboard was bare. Fortunately, there was an egg for Ashley's supper, but the soldiers were complaining of hunger and so I went out into the darkness to search for food. As I walked through the streets I bit down on my lip to keep from sobbing as I stepped around and over soldiers: exhausted soldiers who slept face down in their own vomit and waste; wounded soldiers who bled rivers of blood; and pain-wracked soldiers who reached their hands towards me. I steeled myself not to pause and help those wretched men, for I had taken responsibility for the soldiers sheltering in my home and they were in desperate need of food.

The shops that were still open were stripped of all food, so I knocked at the back doors of hotels and begged bread, but I was turned away empty-handed. In my search I walked through alleys and soon I was lost in a maze of narrow streets. Frightened by a wild dog, I ran in terror and found myself in a dark lane that led towards a small church. A lantern, burning in the doorway, beckoned me inside.

A Roman Catholic priest was kneeling at the altar; in his hands was a string of black beads. Hearing me, he pushed to his feet and asked, "May I help you, my child?"

I apologized for taking him away from his prayers, but he said, "I will finish saying the Rosary later . . . you look in need of help."

In a rush of words I told him about the soldiers sheltering in my house and how I had become lost in my search for food and he led me to his own kitchen where he filled a sack with vegetables and tinned meats (he left only a small crust of bread for himself). Then, guiding me to a main street, he blessed me and we parted—he, to minister to wounded and dying soldiers and I, to nourish hungry and thirsty soldiers.

When I arrived at the house, Ashley seemed less feverish as she slept peacefully, so Charleen and I prepared the food and fed the famished soldiers. Later, as I carried a bucket of water around to the men I realized that they had another need: the rags that bound their wounds were drenched with blood. So, as soon as time allowed, I pulled the sheets from my bed and tore the cloth into long strips. Then, while I wound the strips of cloth into bandages I thought of my sister Julia—she had told me of her frustration to help the wounded after the Battle of Bull Run and how she had discovered that merely listening to the soldiers as they spoke helped them cope with their misery.

So, as I knelt by the soldiers and wrapped their wounds, I listened. Simply listened. And while I listened I began to understand that the soldiers of the Confederacy were no different from the soldiers of the Union. They too, believed in their principles, and they, too, were brave, honorable men. As I listened, some of the soldiers died in my arms, and others grasped my hands as they prepared to die, while still others spoke of their determination to heal so as to return to battle.

*****

About two in the morning, I knew the dead bodies had to be removed before the morning heat came and the smell of rotting flesh sickened the air. I had no choice but to go out into the streets again to search for soldiers who were willing to carry out the dead. Minutes after the bodies were removed, another twenty wounded soldiers took the place of the dead soldiers and those wretched men needed water and food and someone to listen to as they spoke about their families, their pain and their hopes.

*****

As the hours crawled by, the house acquired a deathly quiet except for the occasional moans of the wounded who felt pain in their sleep. Though it was quiet, sleep escaped me, so I sat in the kitchen and cut strips of cloth into bandages. My eyes felt heavy with fatigue, but I kept glancing at the door hoping to hear Hugh's step.

Near three o'clock the front door opened and shut softly and I leapt from my chair and ran down the hall; Hugh was leaning against the door, his suit and shoes wet with blood. He smiled at me, a weary smile, before walking upstairs and by the time I had prepared a pot of tea and a plate of sweet potatoes, he came downstairs wearing a clean suit. While he ate I looked away, for his fingernails were encrusted with dried blood; it sickened me to think of the horrors he had witnessed as a battlefield surgeon.

I poured him another cup of honeyed tea, but he forgot to drink when he began to speak. He said, "Louisa, both the North and the South are claiming victory in the first day of this battle. The Union is calling it the Battle of Fair Oaks while the Confederates are calling it the Battle of Seven Pines. I call it by one name only: Slaughter. Human slaughter."

Hugh sounded as though he were in a trance when he asked, "What day is this, Louisa?"

"Near dawn . . . on Sunday, June 1."

He rubbed his hand across his eyes and said, "Is it possible that all that madness only happened a few short hours ago? Yesterday morning—it seems years ago—I walked with the soldiers down roads and through fields that were knee-deep with water from the flood. Wreckage from the bridges of the Chickahominy littered the surrounding fields, so it was difficult to walk without pushing aside planks and logs.

"Sometime after the noon hour the Confederates blasted their cannons and I swear, Louisa, in that one second thousands of Confederates charged against the Federals. The noise was deafening—the roaring of cannons, the screaming of voices, the cracking of the rifles, the beating of drums, the blowing of bugles—I carried no weapon, so I stood aside and waited for the wounded. I didn't have long to wait."

Hugh pushed to his feet and paced back and forth as he continued, "The fighting took place between two points a mile wide—between Seven Pines and Fair Oaks. I know that land well—there are thick, dark woods that enclose that whole area. During the battle, as far as the eye could see, those woods were hooded by puffs of smoke—smoke from the guns of both Northern and Southern cannon. The smoke added to the mass confusion, but the Confederates were led by generals who are supposedly competent—men named John Gordon, James Longstreet, D. H. Hill, G. W. Smith and Benjamin Huger. They had to fight on that swampy land around the Chickahominy, but their men followed bravely and without hesitation."

Hugh stopped pacing and looking at me he said, "The Federals fought courageously, too. Every time the Confederates pushed them back into the swamp, the Federals returned fire with deadly accuracy. Such courage. Such chaos. Such horror as men and horses fell everywhere onto the watery earth.

"For those first few hours I moved amongst the fallen soldiers and propped them up against rocks or trees to keep them from drowning. Many, too many, drowned where they fell because they didn't have the strength to push their heads above the water."

I sat quietly while Hugh spoke, for it was obvious that he needed to speak of the day's terrors.

He said, "Around noon I was taken to a farmhouse on Chimborazo Hill—the house had been taken over as an aid station for the wounded. I cleared off the kitchen table to use for my surgery . . . no, for my butchery . . . that is what this War has forced me to become . . . a butcher of men. For hours, soldiers were carried in and dropped on the table and then, God forgive me, the only thing I could do was to take my saw and hack off their legs or arms or feet or hands . . . I tried not to look at their faces or listen to their screams . . . some begged me to stop sawing, but I couldn't stop . . . after awhile there were so many legs and arms on the floor that I threw them out a window . . . but the pile of limbs grew so high that it blocked the light from the window.

"When darkness came, the battle ceased . . . on both sides, Union and Confederate, the soldiers merely collapsed on the ground and slept. I left the farmhouse . . . I needed fresh air because the stench of blood and flesh had overwhelmed me. I began to walk . . . all around me were sleeping soldiers . . . they slept amongst the dead . . . the dead of the North and the dead of the South . . . the only way I could tell a wounded man from a dead man was that the wounded cried out for water, but there was no water fit for drinking. Those anguished cries surrounded me, but I could do nothing more. I walked away from those fields of death until I found myself standing on the porch step. I knew Louisa, that you would be here . . . waiting for me."

His words moved my heart; his words warmed my heart. I flew into Hugh's arms and he held me close and taking my face between his hands he looked long into my eyes before pressing his lips against mine. His kiss was passionate, desperate, as though he feared that our first kiss would be our only kiss. In a tormented voice he whispered, "Dawn will come soon. I must return to Chimborazo Hill." Then, once more, he kissed me with sweet passion before walking through the door.

I stood on the step and looked out into the darkness of early morning, but he was gone as though the very air had swallowed him up. I touched my mouth. The warmth of his gentle kiss was still on my lips. I smiled. My heart had lost its numbness; my heart welcomed love.

How long I stood there I can't say, but all of a sudden I realized that soldiers were pleading for water. I picked up the bucket and hurried down the hall.

Just as the clock chimed the hour of four I knelt by the last soldier, a freckle-faced boy named Danny who claimed he was eighteen years though he looked no older than ten years. I held a dipper of water to his mouth and he drank, but then a spasm of coughing came over him and I lifted his head to give him ease. As he coughed he spat bits of blood. I offered him more water, but he shook his head and asked, "Could you write a letter for me?" I smiled and asked him who he wished to write to and his smile widened when he said, "My mama," and then, in that very same moment, he died.

I'm not sure how long I stared down at his child's face before gently closing his eyes. Somehow I pushed myself to my feet, and as though deafened, I walked past the soldiers who called out to me. Slowly, so slowly, I walked upstairs to the darkened room where Charleen and Ashley slept and then, laying on my bed, I pressed my face into my pillow and wept.

*****

When I awoke Charleen and Ashley were gone and a strange feeling of foreboding came over me. Rushing downstairs I found them in the kitchen sitting before the cold hearth. Ashley looked ill, very ill, and that feeling of doom that I had awoken with washed over me and I knew she was dying. She laid quietly in her mother's arms; the circles under her eyes had darkened and her tiny face was flushed and spotted with perspiration.

In a strangled voice Charleen begged, "Please find my brother," and I bolted through the door and out into the street—I ran east towards Chimborazo Hill.

The sun had not yet risen, but there were many afoot as soldiers limped towards Richmond while civilians walked towards the hills that overlooked yesterday's battlefield. Though my side ached I ran until I reached the foot of Chimborazo Hill where a soldier directed me towards a farmhouse that was marked as an aid station. I prayed as I ran up the hill that Hugh would be there.

A few yards away from the farmhouse I was overcome by a terrible stench—under the open window was a pile of human legs and arms and feet; droves of black flies buzzed around the bloody pile. I froze, unable to take another step as a bleeding leg was thrown through the window onto the pile. I doubled over, nauseated by the sight and smells of amputated limbs, but Ashley was depending on me and so I forced myself to run past the gruesome pile and knock at the door.

A man wearing a blood-smeared apron told me that Hugh had been summoned to the top of the hill to attend the governor's secretary who had been kicked by a horse. I ran on.

A mob of hundreds of civilians had gathered at the crest of the hill. Frantic, I looked around for Hugh . . . I saw the governor and President Davis and his ministers standing about in small groups and I saw ladies and clergymen and business men and newspaper reporters—all of them waiting for the battle to resume—but I didn't see Hugh.

Looking wildly about I sobbed aloud with relief when I spotted him sitting behind a man, sewing up his head. Pushing my way through the crowd I gasped, "Hugh, you must come home. Ashley's dying."

Hugh hardly glanced at me. I thought he hadn't heard me, but then he snipped the thread and dropping the needle and scissors into his bag he grabbed my arm and started pulling me down the hill. I stumbled trying to keep up with him and pleading with him to leave me behind, he ran on alone.

I leaned against a tree to rest for a moment as the sun began to show itself in the sky. At that very moment the morning quiet was broken by an explosion. I jerked around. The battle had resumed. Another shell exploded in the air and the branches of the tree shook above me, raining down leaves. Terrified, I ran as the noises of war surrounded me: the roar of cannons, the screams of horses, the blasts of rifles and the slap of shoes as panic-stricken civilians followed me down the hill.

*****

When I arrived back home I found Charleen washing the fever waters from Ashley's face. Hugh had already returned to the aid station, but he had given Ashley a dosage of medicine and had left behind a bottle of greenish-yellow stuff that smelled like moldy cheese.

Ashley looked so fragile; her skin seemed transparent and the circles under her closed eyes looked like smudges of coal. She moaned softly as she drifted in and out of fitful sleep and I suspected she suffered delirium. I placed another basin of wet rags near Charleen, but there was little else I could do except pray—I prayed, too, that Charleen would keep her sanity, for her daughter needed a mother's care. As I watched Charleen I glimpsed again the sort of mother she had once been before this War had sickened her mind.

Shortly after the noon hour the news that the battle had ended spread through Richmond as rapidly as fire spreads over paper. I went upstairs to tell Charleen, but she turned a deaf ear because the battle no longer concerned her. Her only concern was her daughter. I left them together and returned downstairs to care for the soldiers.

Around midnight Ashley's fever broke. Indescribable joy danced over Charleen's face and we hugged each other and cried and laughed. Two hours later the fever faded completely away and I felt certain that Ashley would fully recover. I also began to hope that the crisis had healed Charleen's sick mind, for throughout those tense hours she never slipped into that other world where her husband still lived.

Afterwards, I made my rounds of the soldiers and then slept for a few hours in a kitchen chair, but I woke when I heard a click as the front door closed— Hugh had arrived home from Chimborazo Hill. He went upstairs to change his blood-soaked clothes while I went upstairs to wake Charleen. Before long Hugh was standing beside Ashley's crib, confirming our hope that she was out of danger. Rejoicing, Charleen stayed near her daughter, while Hugh and I went downstairs to the kitchen.

He sat wearily in the rocking chair while I poured him hot coffee, but he was too tired to drink. He took my hand in his and said, "Louisa, as much as I don't want you to leave Richmond, I have found some information that should prove important to Mr. Lincoln's generals. General Joe Johnston is recovering from his wounds in the home of a friend who lives on Church Street—at first his command was taken over by a general named Smith, but by the end of the battle Smith was replaced by General Robert E. Lee as commander of the Confederate armies. You must return to Washington at once—make them understand that General Lee is the singlemost threat to Union success. Convince the War Department that Lee is brilliant, ruthless and fearless—he could lead the Confederacy to a victory."

Hugh's eyes closed briefly, but he shook his head as though to wake himself before saying in a voice hoarsened by exhaustion, "General Lee has made it clear that he will not surrender Richmond without a fight. To strengthen the defense of Richmond, General Lee plans to build up the earthworks surrounding this city."

Hugh removed a paper from his pocket and unfolding it he placed the paper before me; it was a map of Richmond; penciled sketches of massive earthworks were drawn over the perimeter of the city. He explained, "This afternoon when I amputated the leg of an officer this map fell from his pocket . . . it's a copy of General Lee's plans to fortify this city. Take the map to Mr. Lincoln. His generals will make good use of it . . . there must be a flaw in Lee's defense that will enable the Federals to invade this city . . ." Hugh's eyes closed again, but this time they remained closed; he had fallen asleep in an instant. I doused the candles and went upstairs.

I tiptoed past Charleen who tossed restlessly in her bed. The lamp on the desk was dim, but there was enough light to take out my journal and tuck the map under the binding. Then, after hiding the journal in a drawer, I turned down the lamp and laid on my bed. My eyes closed at once.

*****

I woke near dawn and watched through my window as ambulances rolled into sight. Behind the wagons came soldiers; some limped, some staggered and some dragged themselves up the street. Many were blackened—perhaps with gunpowder and dried blood. I watched until I couldn't bear to watch any longer and walking quietly past Charleen and Ashley, I went out into the streets to search for food.

Most of the shops had been emptied of food, but a shopkeeper told me that bread was being sold on the roof tops of buildings.

On the roof of a grand hotel I looked eastwards and saw the grey smudge of the thousands of tents that sheltered McClellan's soldiers. In the distant skies giant spying balloons floated between the clouds and somewhere, faraway, cannons boomed. Looking across the distant miles I wondered where Hugh was at that very moment, but my thoughts were interrupted by the merchant who demanded money for the bread he had placed in my sack.

*****

For the remainder of that day when we weren't tending to the soldiers and looking in on Ashley, Charleen and I sat in the parlor sewing the crude mattresses that Hugh and his fellow surgeons needed for their gruesome surgeries. As evening fell I opened a window and we listened to sorrowful dirges as processions of flower-strewn coffins passed by.

Around midnight Charleen went upstairs to check on Ashley, while I made one last round of the soldiers to give them pieces of bread and water. Then, although I longed for sleep, I noticed that the basket of clean bandages was empty and so I sat down to cut cloth into long strips. At some point I must have drifted off to sleep, because I woke suddenly, startled by the chiming of the hall clock. I tried to push myself up from the chair, but weariness kept me from moving and I closed my eyes again even while I listened to heavy footsteps approaching me. Forcing my eyes open I looked up into Charleen's face; her face was distorted with anger.

She held my journal in her hands and the wild fury in her eyes told me that she had read my notes. Fear muted me as I grabbed at the journal, but Charleen proved quicker than I and pushed me roughly away. In a crazed voice she spat, "You villain. You traitor. How dare you come into my home and spy on me and my husband. When he returns from the battle he'll arrest you and we'll both watch you hang as a spy."

I lost all hope of reasoning with her, for Charleen's mind had not been healed as I had hoped; she had slipped back into that other world where her husband was still alive. To calm her I said, "Mrs. Beecham, I'll wait for your husband to return as you wish—" but she slapped me hard across my face. Tears blurred my eyes and I fully expected another slap, but she stepped away from me as though I were a vile disease. Reaching backwards she snatched at a vase on the mantle and threw it; the vase shattered on the wall behind me. Enraged, she screamed, "Traitor! Traitor!" and then, turning to the mantle for another weapon, her hand found the sword.

She pulled the sword off its hooks and facing me, she pointed the blade at my heart. In a raspy voice she whispered, "I shall kill you myself. Peter will be proud of me."

I stared at the gleaming edge of the blade and its razor-sharp tip and then I looked into Charleen's crazed eyes. Her madness had twisted her mind beyond all reason. Pushing a chair between us, I ran through the door and towards the staircase.

Lifting my skirts I ran up the steps; behind me Charleen muttered vile obscenities as she slashed the sword at my back. I reached the second floor and stared down the empty hallway of closed doors. Behind the doors were wounded soldiers, but most were too weak to help me. I knew I couldn't go upstairs for Ashley would be in danger as well—too often when Charleen slipped into that world of insanity she mistook Ashley for my child. So I turned and waited for Charleen, determined to reason with her.

Slowly she came up the steps, the sword held out towards me as she shouted, "Yankee woman. Yankee spy. You must be punished."

Down the hall a door opened and a Confederate officer who had lost an eye stepped out into the hallway.

He leaned weakly against the wall, and I knew he didn't have the strength to assist me. Why should he? Charleen was shouting that I was a villainous Yankee and as he listened, the expression on his face changed from puzzlement to hatred.

Charleen stepped closer to me, her voice even louder, her insults more threatening as she shook the journal at me. Another door opened and a major who had suffered a leg wound limped out before slumping to the floor. Startled, Charleen jerked around and for the briefest moment the sword dropped to her side. In that very second I lifted my skirts and pushed past her down the steps. Behind me Charleen screamed, "Stop! Spy! Dog! Stop!" But I ran even faster down the steps, for the front door had opened as Hugh walked in.

I threw my arms around him and sobbed, "Charleen knows . . . she has my journal . . . she's trying to kill me with Peter's sword."

We looked up at the top of the landing where Charleen stood, sword upraised in one hand, the journal in her other hand. She shouted, "Don't let her escape, brother dear, for she is a traitor and must suffer." And then, lunging down the steps, her feet tangled in her skirts and she fell.

I held my breath as Charleen pitched down the long staircase until she struck the bottom step with such force that her head snapped backwards. She laid without moving, her back oddly curved, her neck grotesquely twisted, her thin hands stubbornly clutching the sword and journal. The whiteness of her skin and the wideness of her eyes lent her the appearance of a porcelain doll. A broken porcelain doll. She stared at me. There was no expression in her eyes. Charleen was dead.

Violent shudders overcame me as Hugh knelt by his sister and then all at once he grabbed my arm and pulled me up the steps, up past the soldiers who called out questions, up to my chamber where he shut and locked the door. Miraculously, Ashley was still asleep, so Hugh whispered, "Louisa, you must leave before one of those soldiers reports you . . . there are angry mobs of civilians roaming the streets searching for Unionists to hang from trees. I must take you and Ashley away from Richmond."

Puzzled, I looked up at him and he said, "You must take Ashley with you. I've lost my sister. I can't allow my niece to die, too. Sooner or later Richmond will be put under siege and Ashley would starve to death. Please. Take her with you."

I didn't hesitate in giving him my answer, for I loved Ashley dearly. Tenderly, I lifted the sleeping child and then a thought came to me. "Hugh," I whispered, "Charleen showed me her Bible—inside the cover is Ashley's certificate of birth—bring that and the golden heart locket from her sewing basket—one day Ashley will treasure her parents' portraits." He did as I asked and within minutes we were retracing our steps downstairs past the excited soldiers and past Charleen. At the door Hugh removed his coat and returning to his sister he covered her face before taking my journal from her outstretched hand.

We fled east in Hugh's carriage towards the battlefield and no one questioned us because we were mistaken for a doctor and his nurse on their way to help the wounded; indeed, a doctor's bag is truly a passport. Several miles out of Richmond we entered the battlefield, an expanse of scarred land that smelled of death: the smells of the decaying corpses that leaned against trees; the smells of mangled horses that laid in their own waste as they snorted mucous from their nostrils; the smells of gunpowder and cannon smoke. Those smells of death nauseated me, but it was the sight of the injured, bleeding men and the sounds of their moans as they pleaded for help or begged for death that made me curse war.

We drove for what seemed forever through the remnants of the Confederate army, until we came upon the remnants of the Union army. There we smelled the same smells, and saw the same sights and heard the same sounds of death. After awhile I closed my eyes and pressed my face against Ashley who slept quietly in my arms as the carriage rolled on.

After an eternity of time Hugh pulled his carriage behind a Union field hospital; he disappeared into the tent for a long while and returned with an officer named Major E. J. Allen who gave his assurance that he would conduct Ashley and me safely to the War Department in Washington. Then, for a brief moment, Major Allen stepped away to allow us a moment of privacy to speak our farewells.

As Hugh hugged Ashley I saw on his face that he doubted he'd see her again and then he took me into his arms and kissed me with the tenderness of a final good-bye. My tears blinded me as I whispered, "This is not good-bye, Hugh . . . I'll wait for you."

*****

This morning, when Ashley and I arrived in Washington, D.C. by boat, Major Allen escorted me to the Executive Mansion where I met with Mr. Stanton, the Secretary of War. Mr. Stanton expressed interest in my journal entries about the submarine tests and great interest in the map of General Lee's defensive plans for Richmond. At the end of our interview he promised that both Dr. Gleason and Mr. Jones would be arrested as traitors.

It was such a lovely day that I decided to walk home. Indeed, the fresh air brought the roses back to Ashley's cheeks and her eyes shone brighter as she looked about at the wonders of Washington.

As I opened the gate of my home Ashley struggled out of my arms and toddled after a butterfly that flitted into the garden. It pleased me to see her at play again and as I shut the gate I noticed my sister sitting on the bench under the rose trellis; Julia sat with her head lowered and I knew her thoughts were deep, for she was unaware of my presence until I touched her shoulder.

Julia had been crying; her tears told me that James had rejected her loving heart. As we hugged each other she asked me a thousand questions: where had I been, why hadn't I written, why had I lost weight and grown my hair long and so on and so on. Smiling, I tucked my arm through hers and leading her into the garden I said, "Julia, we have much to tell each other, but first there is someone you should meet."

AUTHOR'S NOTE

Perhaps war is mankind's cruelest invention. The Civil War, like all of America's wars, imposed unfathomable misery on our nation, for all of our citizens were involved in the conflict in one of three roles: through military service under the flags of the Union or the Confederacy; through civilian service as healers, factory workers, merchants, entertainers, writers, engineers, and farmers; or through secret service as spies (agents of espionage or counterespionage), raiders or saboteurs. The major characters in this book represent each of these three roles: General Robert E. Lee and General George B. McClellan and their soldiers represent the military; Charleen Beecham, Ashley, and Dr. Hugh Ryle represent the civilians; while Louisa Holmes, Dr. Gleason, Mr. Jones, Major Robert Petrie, and Major E. J. Allen represent the secret service.

At the start of the Civil War neither the Union nor the Confederacy had spy networks in operation. And yet, even before Abraham Lincoln arrived in Washington to take his seat in the Executive Mansion, his life was saved by Union spies, including Allan Pinkerton who is featured in this book under his assumed name, Major E. J. Allen. As the war progressed, the number of spies increased dramatically. Consequently, as the number of spies increased, their methods became more inventive and their equipment became more sophisticated. One device of espionage depicted in this book (see illustration on page 75) is the circular disk with two alphabetical wheels; the Confederacy used the disks to translate secret codes.

It should be noted that the actual spies mentioned in this book are presented as factually as possible: Mr. Jones, the Confederate sympathizer who rowed spies across the Potomac; the Doctor's Line, a ring of Northern doctors who were Confederate spies (of which the fictitious character Dr. Gleason is a member); the notorious spy Rose O'Neal Greenhow; the spymaster Allan Pinkerton; the courageous spy Timothy Webster; and his brave associate Hattie Lawton. All in all, Northern and Southern spies differed in personality and technique, but they shared similar traits: dedication to cause, sheer courage, and in most cases, supreme intelligence.

The year of 1862 is remembered for the Peninsular Campaign: the Federals' failure to capture the Confederates' capital city of Richmond, Virginia, which would have brought about an early end to the bloody war.

As the year, 1862, opened, two generals may have been unaware that they would oppose each other for much of the spring and summer. Those generals were the Southerner Joseph E. Johnston, the commander of the Confederate Army of Northern Virginia, and the Northerner George B. McClellan, the commander of the Federal Army of the Potomac.

General Johnston's army had been the victorious force at the First Battle of Bull Run on July 21, 1861.

At the open of 1862 Johnston's army was still camped at Centreville, in northern Virginia, approximately twenty-five miles from Washington, D.C.

Meanwhile, in Washington, General McClellan was content to parade his army in endless drills around the city. President Abraham Lincoln was at first impatient but eventually angered by his general's inactivity and on February 22, 1862, he issued his first War Order mandating that McClellan move against the enemy.

On March 9, 1862, the tiny Federal ironclad, the U.S.S. *Monitor*, battled the giant Confederate ironclad the C.S.S. *Virginia* (popularly known as the *Merrimack*). Although there was no clear victory in this historic naval battle, the *Monitor* succeeded in preventing the *Merrimack* from destroying Mr. Lincoln's naval fleet at Hampton Roads, Virginia. In addition, the *Monitor* kept the Union's blockade of Confederate ports in operation which in essence prevented Europe from supplying the Confederacy with much needed supplies for its military and citizenry.

Heeding Mr. Lincoln's War Order, General McClellan finalized his plans: he would transport his army by water to the tip of the Virginian peninsula and then march his army up the peninsula to Richmond where he hoped to lay siege to the Confederates' capital city. He believed that General Johnston would have no choice but to follow him and thus the move would eliminate any real threat of Confederate invasion of Washington. Lincoln had another plan in mind, but he agreed with McClellan's strategy. However, since he mistrusted his general he removed him as commander of all Federal armies and took on that responsibility himself (Lincoln remained the commander until 1864 when he found a general he could trust—General Ulysses S. Grant).

On March 26 McClellan marched his massive army out of Washington towards Alexandria, Virginia. His plan was kept secret, for several reasons, one of which was the dangerous presence of spies in Washington. Mrs. Rose Greenhow, a spy for the Confederacy, had already been credited with the loss of the First Battle of Bull Run (the information she smuggled to the Confederates allowed them enough time to reinforce their numbers which led to the defeat of the Federal army). So, for the first time since war had begun, the newspapers did not report the destination and purpose of the Army of the Potomac.

For three days hundreds of ships and boats conveyed the army of 100,000 men, 26,000 horses and mules, 300 cannons, and tons of supplies to the tip of Virginia's peninsula between the two rivers York and James. By the time the final ship had been unloaded, the tents of McClellan's army stretched across the entire width of the peninsula of Virginia.

In the opening days of April, McClellan began to move his army towards his target, Richmond, which lay approximately seventy-three miles up the peninsula. The general moved slowly for he had received erroneous reports from his own spies that he was vastly outnumbered by the Confederates. McClellan's hesitancy was fueled by the fact that Generals Irvin McDowell and Nathaniel Banks could not reinforce him. Their forces were occupied by the brilliant Confederate general, Thomas J. "Stonewall" Jackson, who deliberately distracted and detained the Northern generals in the Shenandoah Valley of Virginia. And so, because McClellan believed himself supremely outnumbered, he inched forward until he reached the Southern line of defense at Yorktown.

The Confederate's line of defense at Yorktown reached across the entire peninsula. McClellan's propensity for caution overwhelmed him. Believing the Confederate's line of defense was heavily manned, he decided against attack. In fact, the Confederate line was sparsely protected; McClellan had been tricked by the Confederate General John B. Magruder who marched the same regiments in and out of different areas to fool McClellan into believing that he faced a superior force.

McClellan's month long delay allowed General Johnston enough time to strengthen his army with an additional 63,000 troops. Meanwhile, farther up the peninsula, Richmond prepared for probable siege by building up the earthworks (small mountains of red soil) around the perimeter of the city. Once the city was considered "safe" General Johnston quietly abandoned Yorktown on the morning of May 3. On the following day General McClellan attacked Yorktown, which by then was meagerly manned by a few thousand Confederates. Afterwards, McClellan proclaimed his taking of Yorktown as a great victory which amused the Confederates.

On May 5 McClellan's forces clashed with Johnston's rear guard at Williamsburg. The Federals suffered high casualties (over 2,000) and the Confederates suffered nearly as many casualties, and yet the Confederates ridiculed Williamsburg as a "fake" battle—supposedly they viewed the conflict as a severe warning to the Federals not to interfere with Confederate withdrawals (indeed, they had managed to withdraw with full supplies).

Regardless of the Confederate's scoffing remarks, McClellan viewed Williamsburg as another victory as he slowly followed Johnston's army towards Richmond. Although the sluggish movement of his army was caused in part by his usual overcaution, the weather also played a part in the army's almost snail-like progress. Thick, knee-deep mud and heavy rains slowed the steps of his soldiers.

As McClellan's troops continued on towards Richmond, the James and York Rivers were trespassed by Union ships. One Federal flotilla was steadily moving up the James River, blasting at riverside plantations and Confederate land batteries. As the flotilla advanced towards Norfolk, the Confederate's Naval Yard, the Southerners had no choice but to abandon their yard. One ship, the mighty ironclad, the *Virginia (Merrimack)*, could not be moved through shallow waters to safety, so to prevent her from being reclaimed by the Federals, the *Merrimack* was filled with explosives and blown up. The crew of the *Merrimack* then boarded a train to Richmond where they would later fight their old enemy, the *Monitor*, on land at Drewry's Bluff.

On May 15 the Federal flotilla reached Drewry's Bluff, only seven short miles outside Richmond. After several hours of battle, the sharpshooters who had concealed themselves at the river's edge and the crew of the *Merrimack* who had manned massive cannons on the bluff, turned back the flotilla. That same evening and for days afterwards the citizens of Richmond rejoiced jubilantly, for their beloved city had been saved.

Since the Federals' plan to conquer Richmond by water had failed, McClellan had to move aggressively against Richmond—if he could take Richmond, the Confederates would lose their capital city and thus the war would speedily end.

Towards the end of May, McClellan's army approached within seven miles of Richmond. Part of his army crossed the Chickahominy River, a foul river that was swollen by the unusually heavy spring rains. On the night of May 30 a violent storm struck. Lightning killed several Federals, the Chickahominy flooded its banks, and the bridges spanning the river were destroyed. To make matters worse, some of McClellan's forces were separated from the rest of his army by the flooding waters of the river. Confederate spies reported the chaos the storm had caused in the Federal camp and many Confederates concluded that heaven had sent the storm upon their enemy.

Johnston planned a morning attack against the Federals who were isolated on the southern side of the river. However, there was some confusion and misdirection and it was around noon before General James Longstreet attacked and pushed the Federal left flank back through the town of Seven Pines. The Federals met the attack bravely even though they were vastly outnumbered and even though they had battled the drowning waters of the river all night which had left them exhausted beyond all measure. The repulsion of the Federals ended when they were reinforced by Edwin Sumner's II Corps who had managed to cross the river. The Confederates' assault was finally stopped at Fair Oaks.

An event of momentous importance happened as the first day of battle neared its end: General Joseph E. Johnston was gravely wounded and carried by stretcher to Richmond. Johnston was placed in the home of a friend where he would eventually recover from his wounds. However, before the end of the next day, Robert E. Lee would be named in Johnston's place as the army's new commander. The change in command would have dire consequences for the North: Lee would become the singlemost threat to the Union's goal of victory—reunification with the South as a whole nation.

Throughout the hours of the first night of battle, Confederate wounded and dead were conveyed into Richmond where the citizens tended to their needs as best they could in spite of their own impoverished situations.

On the following day, at the break of dawn, the Confederates launched another attack, but much confusion ensued. By battle's end the North had more than 5,000 casualties, while the South suffered even more, over 6,000 casualties.

In a war in which retreat spelled defeat, there were no losers in the battle that the Northerners called Fair Oaks and the Southerners called Seven Pines. The Confederates saw victory in that their city had not yielded to their enemy and McClellan claimed victory in that he still camped outside the city. Neither side had earned real victory, for as in the game of chess, they had simply reached a stalemate. And although McClellan would remain on the peninsula for another few weeks of battle he would soon retreat back to Washington with his objective unaccomplished—Richmond would remain the Confederates' capital city for several more years as the terrible war waged on.